Mr. Perfect

Malhotras

A romance novel by

SUNDARI VENKATRAMAN

FLAMING SUN

Notion Press Media Pvt Ltd

No. 50, Chettiyar Agaram Main Road,
Vanagaram, Chennai, Tamil Nadu – 600 095

First published by Flaming Sun 2021
Printed & Distributed by Notion Press
Copyright © Sundari Venkatraman 2023
All Rights Reserved.

ISBN 979-8-88935-855-8

Cover Design by: Vivek Chandanshiv
Beta Read by: Rubina Ramesh
Edited & Marketed by: The Book Club

"Don't," he protested, a shudder taking him unawares.

"Why not?" she whispered in his ear, brushing her lips over the lobe.

Aarav moved away with an effort, staring at her in awe. She looked so young and innocent, but oh so beautiful! "I don't think this is right, Saloni. Shantanu Uncle..."

"...thinks very highly of you. You are his golden boy. Didn't you know that?" Her eyelashes fluttered rapidly against her rosy cheeks as she asked him the question.

Colour ran up Aarav's face. Yes, Shantanu Uncle and Ganga Aunty were too good to him. They had encouraged him to study, even planning to send him abroad to complete his fourth year of BBA and also get an MBA degree. He nodded now. "Yeah. But still..."

"Still what? Don't you like me?" Huge brown eyes looked up at him appealingly.

"That's not the point..."

"Then what is?"

"Saloni, you're a kid. You..."

"Do you really believe it?" Saloni challenged him. "Tell me if you don't like me; I can accept that." Her face turned mutinous.

Aarav was flummoxed. "But that won't be true."

She grinned. "Kiss me then."

ABOUT THE AUTHOR

Sundari Venkatraman is an Indie Author who has 60 books to her credit. These books have consistently featured in the Top 100 Bestseller Lists on Amazon India, Amazon USA, Amazon UK, Amazon Canada and Amazon Australia in both romance as well as Asian Drama categories. Her latest hot romances have all been on #1 Bestseller slot in Amazon India for over a month.

MR. PERFECT is a standalone romance; the heroine belonging to the Delhi branch of Malhotras. This kindle book remained in #1 Bestseller position on Amazon India for more than three months in the Contemporary Romance and Asian Drama categories.

Even as a child, Sundari absolutely loved the 'lived happily ever after' syndrome and she grew up on a steady diet of fairy tales, Phantom comics and Mandrake comics. It was always about good triumphing over evil and a happy ending after the protagonists surmounted all unexpected obstacles.

Once she entered her teens, Sundari switched her loyalties from fairy tales to Mills & Boon. While she loved reading both of these, she kept visualising what would have happened if there were similar situations happening in India; to local heroes and heroines. And of course, the joy of vanquishing the ubiquitous evil villains! Her imagination soared and she happily ensconced herself in a rosy romantic cocoon for many years.

Then came the writing—a true bolt from the blue! And Sundari Venkatraman has never looked back.

Books by Sundari Venkatraman

Standalone novels
The Malhotra Bride
Meghna
The Madras Affair
An Autograph for Anjali
Twin Torment
Finding Anya
Mr. Perfect
Man Friday
Her Prince Charming
Love in Agartha
Arjun's Penance
The Floundering Author
Once Bitten Twice Lucky
Ryan Finds a Bride
Tinder Loving Care
Shaan Gets Hitched
For Better or For Worse
Heartthrob
Call of the Heart
Sing For Me

Collection of shorts
Matches Made in Heaven
Tales of Sunshine

The Groom Series Trilogy
#1 Groomnapped
#2 Gobsmacked
#3 Grounded

Dashavatar (Indian Mythology)
MATSYA: The First Avatar
KURMA: The Second Avatar
VARAHA: The Third Avatar
NARASIMHA: The Fourth Avatar
VAMANA: The Fifth Avatar
PARASHURAMA: The Sixth Avatar

The Writer's Toolkit (Non-fiction)
Publishing Your Book on Amazon
KDP

Marriages Made in India Series
#1 The Runaway Bridegroom
#2 Her Smitten Husband
#3 His Drunken Wife
#4 Her Secret Husband
#5 The Casanova's Wife
#6 Her Bohemian Husband

The Bansal Legacy Trilogy
#1 Simha International
#2 Rose Garden International
#3 Maharaja International

Written in the Stars Series
#1 Scorpio Superstar
#2 Leo's Desire
#3 Taurus Temptation
#4 Virgo's Krush

The Thakore Royals Trilogy
#1 The Marriage Predicament
#2 Tied in Knots
#3 The Wooing of the Shrew

Romantic Shorts
#1 *Chahti Hoon Tumhe*
#2 Beauty is but Skin Deep
#3 Madeinheaven.com
#4 An Arranged Match
#5 The Reluctant Bride
#6 *Shweta ka Swayamvar*
#7 Papa's Girl
#8 Red Rose Dating Agency
#9 Rahat Mili
#10 Reema's Matchmakers
#11 The Matchmaker's Dream

**The Princess Series
(Historical Romance)**
#1 The Passionate Princess
#2 The Rebel Princess

DEDICATION

This special April birthday edition, is for my niece Divya

1

Saloni stepped out of her bedroom at her parents' home in Delhi when she was startled to see her sister Ruma walk across the wide corridor and into the bedroom the latter's fiancé was put up in. Saloni frowned as it was way past midnight, but a smile soon overtook her features. Well, Ruma and her betrothed, Lakshman, were actually married in secret. Yes, she had got to know all about it the moment she had arrived from Chicago a couple of days ago, her husband Manish and six-month-old son Mitesh in tow.

Saloni sighed inadvertently, the depth of yearning for physical contact hitting her so suddenly. Manish was fast asleep, snoring lightly. They had not had sex in six months, not from the time their baby was born. She had tried hinting at first and then even asked him outright, but it looked like her husband was not going to play ball.

"Saloni, have you checked yourself in the mirror recently?" he had asked, a sarcastic smile on his handsome face, "You're as shapely as a pumpkin. Can you blame me for not wanting to have sex with you?"

This was four months after Mitesh was born and Saloni had been craving her husband's touch. It had got lonely after her mother went back to India, confident that Saloni could manage her one-month-old baby since she was a full-time homemaker. Well, she did manage her home and child well; just as well as she took care of her doctor husband, who was perfectly capable of taking care of himself, only he chose not to. But was it too much to expect some adult company and touch? Manish seemed to think so.

Saloni went red, shrinking within herself. She did look into the mirror after he left the house to party with his bachelor friends. Had she become bloated? She turned this way and that but could not see that it was all that bad. Her stomach was flat, same as before the baby was born. Her breasts had filled out, but then, she still breastfed her infant so it was to be expected. Being a little more honest with herself, Saloni admitted that her thighs were thicker than before. But then, motherhood was about all these changes, was it not? And Manish being a doctor, shouldn't he understand it better than the others?

Saloni sighed. Yes, she was a little rounder than before, but she definitely did not resemble a pumpkin.

That conversation had been the end of it. Manish never wanted to make love with her. Saloni had grown so bored with her own company, with no one to talk to—well, she did talk a lot to her infant son, but he only cooed back to her—that she could not wait to get back to Delhi for a break. "I can take only a couple of weeks off. You stay longer if you want to. Just don't forget that I'm not of much use in the kitchen and it would be better to have you back to make my meals. So, don't take too long," was her husband's advice before they boarded their flight to India.

As if her only role in his life was to cook his meals!

Saloni wanted to scream in frustration, her face going red with temper, though she did n0t say anything in response to his firm instruction. That she did not utter the words did not really stop Saloni from thinking them. The few times when she had protested about something or the other, Manish had sulked, refusing to talk to her for many days at a time, making her feel lonelier than ever. The absolute silence during those times had almost driven her up the wall.

Today, Saloni felt envious of her younger sister as she saw Ruma rushing into Lakshman's arms. Was she not lucky?!

A yell sounded a few seconds later, breaking the silence of the tranquil night. Saloni rushed back into her bedroom to see Mitesh sobbing and Manish calling out to her at the top of his voice, not having stirred from his position on the bed. "Where the hell were you? Can't you keep the brat from crying for a few hours? I haven't had a peaceful night's sleep from the day he was born. Tch! One responsibility you have and even that you cannot manage properly."

Could he not see that his shouting only made the baby howl all the more? Saloni lifted Mitesh from his baby cot and held him close to her breast, soothing his back as she spoke to him softly. "No no, sweetheart.

Don't cry." She changed his diaper swiftly before feeding him. Hiccupping softly, Mitesh calmed down, going to sleep as he was dry and well fed by now. Saloni brushed the thick curls back from the baby's forehead, looking at him with love shining in her eyes. For all her marriage was worth, she could never regret it since it had given her little Mitesh.

Aarav Chopra crossed the threshold of the Malhotra home for the first time after Saloni became engaged to Manish Chawla three years ago. That too only because Ganga Malhotra, Saloni's grandmother, had invited him personally for Ruma's wedding. No one refused the matriarch, more because of the affection and respect with which she treated everybody.

His eyes fell on the infant in a pram and he could not resist stepping closer to check the baby out. His steel grey eyes went wide with shock when he noticed Saloni's features imprinted on the baby face. Oh my God! This had to be her child. He looked at the young girl who was in charge and asked, "What's his name?"

"Mitesh," said the girl shyly, eyeing the tall stranger warily.

Aarav went on his knees beside the pram and smiled broadly at the baby, who gave him a toothless grin in response. "Hello, little man." The baby caught hold of the finger which Aarav pointed at him, gurgling with joy, slowly pulling it towards his mouth.

"No no, little man. Not that," laughed Aarav, pulling his hand away from the baby's face. "I don't think so."

Mitesh screwed up his face, getting all set to bawl his lungs out when Aarav lifted him out of the pram to hold him against his chest. "Naughty little man," he said, shaking his head at the baby, touching his finger to the button nose.

Mitesh forgot to cry, gurgling again, his little hand catching hold of a fistful of Aarav's dark hair as the man bent down to bestow a kiss on the tiny forehead. "Ouch," laughed Aarav, as the little one tugged hard.

"Oh my God! I'm so sorry," said Saloni, gently prising the baby fingers off Aarav's hair. She laughed softly, looking up at the man as he lifted his head, a startled look on her face when she recognised him. "If it isn't Aarav Chopra! Where have you been all these years?" She gave him a wide smile, ignoring the tingle she felt in her fingers when they came in contact with his silky hair.

Aarav looked as if he had been punched hard in his solar plexus. Yes, he knew her face; he had even dreamt of it day and night since he had been a little over twenty and she was barely seventeen. But it never failed to hit him—her breath-taking beauty. Her large brown eyes with curling dark eyelashes, her silky soft cheeks which were on the chubbier side, her pert nose which pointed up in the air whenever she raised her head a few inches to look up at him, and her determined little chin—the whole package aroused him painfully while his heart battered against his chest, his stomach churning as it joined the melee. She had put on a bit of weight but it sat well on her five-foot, eight-inch frame, only adding to her womanly shape. But, Aarav sighed, she belonged to another man, one who had fathered this adorable baby.

He smiled now, gulping in the bitter taste of bile, before responding, "Hello Saloni! How have you been? Your little guy is simply gorgeous," he said, bending down to kiss the baby's cheek, only to have his hair caught again by a little fist. "And naughty too," laughed Aarav as the baby's mother pulled the tiny fingers off gently once again. Only, it brought her a little too close for comfort, making Aarav's body tighten with need. He handed the baby to Saloni in a rush, a trifle desperate to get away from her.

Mitesh started crying the moment Aarav let him go. Saloni laughed, patting her son on his back as she placed him on her shoulder. "There, there, Mitesh darling. *So jao*! Come along inside, Aarav. The wedding ceremony should begin any minute," said Saloni, holding him by his arm and pulling him inside the house.

Aarav went, drawn by both the mother and the son. Shit! He was falling in love with her all over again. Why couldn't his heart just accept the fact that she was a married woman and a mother at that? But no, his heart did not seem to care, not one little bit. And this time round, he had not just fallen for Saloni, but her little son too.

"Hello Aarav *beta*, I'm so happy to see you. Thank you for coming at such a short notice," said Ganga, pulling him into a hug when he bent down to touch her feet.

"How have you been, *Daadima*?" he said, hugging her right back. "And from when have you started thanking your grandchildren for showing their affection?" he teased, kissing her on her wrinkled cheek.

Ganga laughed. "As smart and cheeky as ever," she said, taking him by the hand and introducing him to Lakshman, the bridegroom.

Neither Ganga nor her husband Shantanu—who was no more—had ever been bothered by the fact that Aarav's father Tejpal Chopra used to be their driver until the day he retired. It was Shantanu who had recognised the fire in the younger Aarav and had helped him channelise it, ensuring that he got the right kind of education.

Aarav conversed with Lakshman before Ruma arrived and the couple needed to go sit in the *mandap* as the wedding rites began.

Aarav went around, chatting with Akshay and his wife Sunita, paying his respects to Raj and Tanuja Malhotra—all belonging to the Malhotra clan based in Mumbai—before returning to stand next to the pram. He could not help but be fascinated by little Mitesh who cooed at him, lifting his arms and legs up in the air as if in invitation. "What?" Aarav whispered to the baby with a wide grin, "Do you want to pull my hair or do you want to munch on my finger?"

Mitesh gurgled, catching hold of Aarav's finger once again. Saloni arrived just then, holding a man by the hand. "Aarav, I would like you to meet my husband, Dr Manish Chawla. And Manish, this is Aarav Chopra..."

Manish's jaw dropped. "The Aarav Chopra?" he asked in a reverent whisper, his eyes going wide.

Aarav got up from his knees, unable to resist lifting the baby in his arms, and stood tall in front of the other man, disliking him on sight. But then, there was no surprise there. He would have hated anyone who was married to Saloni. Now he nodded, saying, "Yes." He did not even bother to shake the other man's hand, in the pretext of holding baby Mitesh in both his arms.

Saloni looked from one to the other, confused. "What do you mean?" she asked her husband. "Who do you think Aarav Chopra is?" She asked, her hands on her hips.

"Women!" fumed Manish, an impatient expression on his face. "You are an idiot, Saloni! Why don't you read the newspapers some time? Aarav Chopra has single-handedly set up his diverse group of companies and his name is listed among the top hundred richest people in India. Don't tell me you didn't know?" He turned to Aarav and said, "I need a picture of you with my kid, buddy. I promise you that this will go viral on social media." Manish took out his phone and clicked away speedily, not even waiting to find out if the other man was okay with it.

Aarav did not really give a damn, holding Saloni's baby close to his heart as he laughed, saying, "Saloni knows me from a different time, Dr Chawla. Of course! I don't need to tell you that she stood first in the Delhi University during her MBA finals. An idiot couldn't have done that." He walked away, handing little Mitesh to his mother, refusing to be moved by the baby's cries. He needed to get away or he might just choke the life out of Manish Chawla.

3

Saloni was not sure if she hated herself or her husband more as she stood watching him sleeping deeply. She brushed away the tear which fell down her left cheek, only to have another one following it. She was so tempted to smash something or at least scream the place down. But she did not want to wake either of the men in her life. It was a good thing that Mitesh was generally a peaceful baby, crying infrequently. But even those rare occasions triggered off her husband's temper.

What the hell! Saloni fumed as her mind drifted into the happy days of her past, before Manish came into her life...

Saloni Malhotra had been twenty-three and floating on cloud nine when she got to know that she had passed her MBA finals with flying colours. She had always wanted a career, keen to be a mover and shaker in the world of business.

Saloni walked into her home, thrilled to share the wonderful news that she had topped in the university. "Mamma, *Daadima*, I have some awesome news. You know what? I came first." She grinned from ear to ear as her grandmother Ganga swept her into a hug while Rati stood back to watch her with a small frown.

"I'm so proud of you, *beta*. And so would your grandfather be if he had been alive." Ganga kissed her elder granddaughter on her forehead.

"I just can't see the need to study so much," declared Rati, "In the end, you are going to be running someone's home. What a waste of time and money?!"

"How can you say that, Mamma? I have already received three offers from big companies. I'm going to talk to Pappa and maybe I'll also call Akshay *Chachu* and consult him as to which is the best offer. I..."

"Are you mad, Saloni? Just forget it. I've already chosen an excellent NRI groom for you. The Chawlas are coming to see you the day after tomorrow. Manish Chawla is a doctor who is based in the USA and is earning in dollars. You'll have a wonderful life." Rati smacked her lips, excited at the prospect of organising the wedding of her eldest born.

Saloni looked at her mother, her brown eyes opening wide in shock. "Mamma, I want to have a career, not get married. I've just completed my education and I..." She turned to look at her silent grandmother who was watching her daughter-in-law in turn. Ganga never interfered with Rati's decisions, even if she did not agree with most of her views. That way, peace reigned in the family. While Ganga was still working as a consultant at their family business,

Rati preferred to remain a housewife. But Ganga was okay with that. She led her own life, letting Rati lead hers, intervening only on rare occasions, that too, only under dire circumstances.

"Don't be stupid, Saloni. Where's the need for you to earn? By God's grace, we have more than enough. You are already twenty-three years old. People have started asking me why you aren't married yet. I feel ashamed at times, especially when my friends at our kitty parties talk behind my back."

"How would you know if they were talking behind your back?" asked Saloni, sarcasm tingeing her words.

Ganga continued to watch quietly, even though the same question had risen in her mind too.

"Don't you dare talk back to your elders, Saloni. I have already invited the Chawlas and they will be here at 5 pm on the day after tomorrow. Just get yourself prepared to settle down in the USA. You can get married and work there if you want to. I don't think Manish will have a problem with that."

"But Mamma, I'm not interested in shifting to the USA. Why are you forcing me to do this?"

"What nonsense is this? You will have to shift to the USA because that's where your husband is living. Where am I forcing you?" Rati had begun to scream now.

"Can you hear yourself Mamma? I am not married and I have no husband. Why the hell should I shift out of Delhi? I love living here and I don't want to go anywhere else, unless for a holiday." Saloni kept her voice decibel down only out of respect to her grandmother. She was too angry with her mother by now.

"But you will be married, and soon too, if I have my way. Manish is here on leave for twenty days. In fact, he's arriving in Delhi only tomorrow. He will meet you on the very next day. Pappa and I have already spoken to his parents. He has also seen your photo and is keen to marry you. The wedding will need to happen within two weeks and..."

Saloni shuddered. "How long have these talks been going on? Why did you never consult me regarding this?"

"*Aaj kal ke bachhon mein sharam naam ki cheez hai hi nahi,*" declared Rati vehemently. "You were busy with your studies and it's the parents' duty to fix their daughter's wedding. Why should we consult you about this? Don't you have the confidence that we would find the right man for you? My parents never asked me if I wanted to marry your father. I hadn't even spoken to him before our marriage. But then, as I mentioned, we girls in those days were shy about discussing such things. But you people..."

"Spare me the lecture, Mamma. This is beyond irritating." Saloni left the living room abruptly, walking up the stairs of the duplex to rush into her bedroom on the first floor and locking herself inside. She quickly sent a WhatsApp message to her sister Ruma. "Mamma's screwing my life. I need to talk to you desperately. Get home fast and come directly over to my room."

She heard a soft knock on her door about forty-five minutes later and opened it to let Ruma in. "What happened Sal?" Ruma stared at her elder sister whose eyes were red from crying. "I thought you were going out to celebrate your MBA results."

"Ruma!" Saloni fell into her sister's arms, howling. "Mamma has arranged my wedding with some NRI from the US." She went on to repeat everything Rati had told her. "How the hell can I get out of this? I..."

Ruma looked at Saloni, her face pale with shock. "But how can she do that? You want a career, right?"

"Exactly! And how many times do I explain that to her?" Fresh tears rolled down Saloni's cheeks.

"But wait a minute. Maybe, just maybe, we can try to turn this to your advantage. I know you're keen to live in Delhi. But working in the USA can't be bad as so many of our people shift over to build a career there. Why don't you meet this guy first? If you like him, then maybe your life's sorted, though differently from what you had imagined. You know Mamma! She's too stubborn and always gets her own way. Go along with her plans and check this out. With your kind of marks and all that, I don't think you'll have a problem landing a job in Chicago."

Saloni looked at her sister, her tears having dried up by now. She slowly nodded her head. "Yeah, I suppose you're right. It's not a bad idea." She smiled now. "Not a bad idea at all. You're the one with the solutions, Ruma. Thanks." She bumped her fist with her sister's. "Do you want to go out for dinner? My treat!"

"Yes," said Ruma, throwing an arm around her sister.

Manish and Saloni had liked each other on that first meeting. He was smart, good-looking and seemed to have a rocking career at a hospital in Chicago. Saloni made a mistake though. It never struck her to ask him about working opportunities in the USA for an NRI wife. She had presumed that with her qualifications, it would be too easy to land a job of her choice. The two of them were married with the blessings of both their families and Manish returned to the USA, leaving his two-day-old wife behind, to get her papers in order and travel to Chicago at the first opportunity.

In the first few weeks of going to her husband's home, Saloni had been happy with all the socialising they did. Manish had so many friends and colleagues who wanted to invite the newly married couple to their homes. Manish, too, threw parties at every opportunity he got. Saloni was a really good cook and her new husband had been thrilled to show off her skills, throwing parties at every opportunity.

But it all began to wane after a while. Saloni realised two things. First, that it was not so easy going to work in the USA, despite the qualifications that she possessed, because she did not have the right work permit or visa. And secondly—this one she had a tough time admitting even to herself—her husband had never wanted a career woman for his wife. He wanted to show off his well-educated housewife to all the people he knew.

"Manish." They had just made love or rather Manish had had his pleasure with Saloni, not at all bothered if she had been satisfied, when she opened the conversation. "Can't we move to Delhi? We both..."

Manish sat up with a start, glowering at his wife. He had almost gone to sleep when he heard her question. "Are you crazy Saloni? You do know how much I earn here, don't you? I'll never make that kind of money in India. Do you take me for a fool or what?"

Saloni placed a gentle hand on his shoulder, hoping to pacify him. "Manish, you left India more than ten years ago. Things have changed. If you set up a private clinic there and are attached to a hospital too, you can easily make a lot of money. And I can also get a job. Between us, we can make way more than the two of us can spend in our lifetime. Please..."

"Shut up!" Manish panicked. He did not want to go back to India. Today, he spoke so proudly to all his Indian relatives and friends about the rocking life he led in Chicago. What would they all think if he moved back now, and that too just because his wife wanted him to? "Why can't you adjust to our lives here? You did know what you were signing up for when you agreed to marry me, right? You aren't being fair to me Saloni. I've worked so hard, completing my education and setting up my career here, sometimes working twelve to fourteen hours in a day. How dare you try to uproot me at this point in my life?" He had a good mind to slap his wife.

"But Manish, I also worked hard to get my post-grad degree. It's all lying waste now. You know that I can't work here. I..."

"How does it matter? At the end of all this, isn't a woman's place in the kitchen? And listen Saloni, you're such a good cook. Everyone's praising the meals which you turn out, such different cuisines too." Manish smiled, trying to cajole her. But she did not fail to notice that he did not touch her. Manish never hugged her nor were there those tender touches that usually happen between a married couple, especially newlyweds. The only time he got close to within touching distance was when they had sex, which was maybe a couple of times in a week, and that too only when he instigated it. He usually ignored her if Saloni made any overtures. She had eventually given up after trying a few times.

Manish continued to talk, "You keep our home so beautiful and neat. I'll tell you what? Let's have a baby. Then maybe you won't feel so bored. In fact, my mom has been asking me about it every time I call her. She so wants to be a grandmother." He laughed as if he had found the solution to all her problems.

But what a reason to have a baby, just so that she won't be bored! Saloni wanted to scream at her husband or even hit him. She would have done just that, *if* she had believed it would have made a difference to her life.

Saloni came back to the present when she saw Mitesh's face crumble. It was past 2 am and he must be wet. She changed his diaper before feeding him and rocking him to sleep. Pressing her lips to the baby's forehead, she could not help recalling the scene when Aarav had done exactly that.

A deep sigh shuddered through Saloni's being as thoughts of Aarav kept springing forth to the surface of her mind, doing her darnedest to force them right back into the recesses of her mind, without any success. He seemed to have only got handsomer than before. While his hair was as silky as ever. As for his adoring interaction with her baby…

No! Saloni shook her head, holding tightly to her son, like a talisman. She would not let her thoughts go there as that way lay deep pain.

4

It was barely 6.30 in the morning after Ruma's wedding. Aarav jogged more than usual, sweat pouring down his face as he pounded his way around the jogging track in the building complex he resided in at Gurgaon, his mind working furiously. Going to the Malhotra residence had been the first mistake. Connecting with Saloni's infant son had been the second one. Falling all over in love again with…

Aarav stopped suddenly, bending down as his breath came out in gasps, his hands pressed to his knees. He *never* got breathless while jogging, like never. Damn it all to hell! He had believed that he was home safe after pushing the thoughts of Saloni right at the back of his mind, clear that he would never allow them to surface. It had taken but one eye contact to rekindle the raw feelings which he still nurtured for her. His mother had stopped asking him to get married once he made it clear that he did not want to take the responsibility of making another woman unhappy as he could not love anyone else, not after Saloni.

Saloni! Aarav straightened up, a small smile tilting the corners of his mouth as he wiped his face and neck with a hand towel and drank deeply from the bottle of water which he had placed on a bench at the side of the track...

It was a little more than nine years ago when Aarav rang the doorbell of the Malhotras' duplex at about 7.30 in the morning. His eyes went wide as he stared unblinking at the vision which had opened the door for him. The girl must have been in her teens, wearing a sweater over her full-length cotton pyjamas, her hair tousled as if she had just got out of bed. Large, brown eyes stared right back at him, the thick and curling eyelashes fluttering rapidly.

"Who are you?" she had asked him, her voice commanding, a shapely eyebrow rising up to touch her hairline.

"I'm Aarav Chopra. Is Shantanu Uncle home?" he asked, his voice gruff due to his dried-up throat, even while his heart insisted on beating double time.

She turned her head towards inside, a hand still holding the door as if to bar him from entering the flat, and called out, "*Daadaji*, someone is here to meet you."

Shantanu Malhotra stepped out of a room to the side of the living room and lifted a hand in a wave to Aarav, "Aarav *beta, aa jao andhar*. Saloni, ask Vinayak to bring a cup of tea." The old man pointed to a chair, indicating that Aarav should sit down as the latter walked into the living room to stand awkwardly, his arms folded against his chest.

Her name was Saloni! Aarav swallowed, feeling an unfamiliar pressure in his chest. He had never set eyes on a more beautiful young woman in his life.

"*Ji* Uncle," said Aarav, sitting down on the chair.

"How's Tejpal now? Did you take him to a doctor?" asked Shantanu, concern in his voice. He did not notice Saloni turning to stare at the young man, a surprised look on her face.

"Pappa is better, Uncle. Only, the doctor has insisted that he should take bed rest for at least two days. If you don't mind, I can drive you around," suggested Aarav, his voice soft.

Shantanu smiled, patting the younger man's shoulder affectionately. "But won't you need to go to college? I don't want you to take leave unnecessarily."

Aarav looked up at the kind, old eyes and said, "Pappa said that you need to be dropped at your office and picked up in the evening. My college is from noon until 5 pm, Uncle. I can drive you and also attend college."

"Have some tea," said Shantanu when Vinayak, the cook, brought a cup. "Alright then. I'll be ready to leave at 8.30 am."

Aarav nodded. "I'll clean the car if you will give me the keys, Uncle," he said, sipping from the tea cup. It was with great difficulty that he stopped his eyes from straying towards the gorgeous Saloni who still stood at the back of the living room, obviously listening to the conversation.

"Sure," said Shantanu. Saloni rushed forward with the car keys even before her grandfather could ask for them.

"Here," she offered the keys to Aarav.

Aarav felt something akin to a bolt of lightning when his fingers brushed against Saloni's as he took the keys from her. He got up with a jerk. "Can you show me the wash basin? Let me wash my tea cup."

"Leave it on the table, Aarav," said Shantanu.

Aarav nodded, turned around and left, his heart pounding.

He shook his head to himself several times while he washed the black Mercedes car. It was sheer idiocy to fall for Shantanu Uncle's granddaughter Saloni, who was way out of his reach. He was, after all, their driver's son. With a deep sigh, Aarav left the compound, unable to resist taking a peek towards the duplex which was set on the tenth and eleventh floor of the building. It was only thanks to Shantanu Malhotra that Aarav was getting a chance to study. His father, Tejpal, had been working as their driver over the last eighteen years and though he was paid well, he could not have afforded to give his children the kind of education they were getting. At twenty-one, Aarav was in the final year of his Bachelor of Business Administration course at the Delhi University. And even this was possible only because Shantanu and Ganga Malhotra had taken a keen interest in Tejpal's family, ensuring that his children received at least basic education.

Aarav came back to the present when he heard the ring of a cycle bell. He smiled and waved at the kid who was riding on the path parallel to the jogging track before walking over to a private lift. He opened it with an electronic key card before getting in and pressing the only button that would whisk him to the twenty-fifth floor, directly into the living room of the penthouse where he resided. He lived all alone in the apartment which covered the whole of the top floor of the building, unless you counted the manservant, Baldev, who lived in the staff quarter half a floor below. Baldev hailed from Aizawl in Mizoram and ran Aarav's home on oiled wheels, taking the cooking and cleaning in his stride.

Aarav entered his home to be greeted by the soft music of a *bhajan* which automatically brought a smile to his face. Oh yes, his mother Amrita had trained Baldev well. While Aarav was not exactly a fan of devotional music, his mother was convinced that listening to it in the morning would help him stay grounded. And he had gotten so used to doing exactly that that he missed it during the times he travelled.

Pouring himself a cup of coffee from the flask which was placed on the centre table in the living room, Aarav sat down on the luxurious sofa to read the newspaper. It was the business and the entertainment sections which interested him more than the front pages which screamed of bomb blasts, accidents and politics gone berserk.

Aarav got ready and left for work at 8.30 am after having his breakfast. All this he did automatically, his mind revolving around Saloni and Mitesh. And he refused to dwell on her husband.

Parking his less-than-a-month-old, dark blue, Mercedes-Benz E-Class car in the place marked for the company president, Aarav walked into the five-floor building which housed one of his company's— *AC Events*—offices, and took the stairs to his office on the top floor. Soon, he immersed himself so completely in his work that he had no bandwidth to dwell on Saloni.

5

aloni, Manish, Ruma and Lakshman went out for dinner on the evening after the wedding. "Manish, shall we take Mitesh along? He so loves going out and enjoys company too. He won't be any trouble in his pram..."

"Are you mad, woman?" Manish snarled at his wife, eyeing her with disgust in his eyes. "Won't your son stay without you for even a couple of hours? It is only in Chicago that we can't leave him back every time we go out."

No, she did not point out that he never took her with him whenever he went out in Chicago; not even once after Mitesh was born.

"Why the hell can't he stay home with your parents and grandmother, now that we're here in Delhi? And then there's that girl Bindi to take care of him too." He turned away muttering loud enough for her to hear, "I don't know what the hell I ever saw in you! We can't seem to have an adult outing, ever."

Saloni turned red; her hands fisting tightly as she held back her temper. It was no use losing it. Manish would only ensure that the evening turned into a complete disaster. And she simply could not do it to the newlyweds. Ruma and Laki looked so happy. She walked out of the bedroom to go meet her son, who was in her grandmother's room.

"*Daadima*, is it okay if I leave Mitesh with you? I..."

Smiling, Ganga looked up from the cradle where she had been chatting with her great grandson. "Of course, Saloni. Do you have to ask?" Noticing her granddaughter's red face, she asked, "Is something wrong, *beta*?"

Saloni refused to meet Ganga's eyes as she shook her head, bending down to speak to her son, "Mitesh baby, Mamma's going out for a while. Will you be a good boy?" she said, kissing him on his forehead.

Mitesh gurgled, kicking his arms and legs, reaching out little fingers to catch hold of a dangling earring. His mother moved her head away, laughing at him as she waved a finger. "No, no, you naughty little guy! See you soon, my baby," she whispered, before getting up to go. Saloni did not notice the strange look which her grandmother gave her as she left the room.

Lakshman drove the car after the four of them settled in. "Rather you than me, bro," said Manish, "I can't imagine driving in this crazy traffic. You know, in Chicago..."

Saloni tuned off, looking out of her window to check out the Delhi crowd that she loved so much. She decided to soak in the atmosphere as much as she could since she had barely another three weeks to go before she returned to the USA. And she was in no mood to listen to her husband prattling on and on about Chicago. It was not as if she disliked the American city, only that she hated the loneliness which kept her company while there. Even the closest neighbours in the apartment block they lived in, were strangers to her. The only people she knew were her husband's colleagues and friends, but Manish had made it obvious that he was not happy if she socialised with them.

Ruma had booked a table at On the Waterfront, a restaurant in Lodhi Road. They reached there at 8.30 pm and were shown to a table for four with comfortable seating. Manish continued to regale Lakshman with anecdotes of his life in Chicago while Saloni and Ruma chatted quietly between themselves. All the while, Saloni could not help but notice Lakshman refusing to let go of his new wife's hand, even as their eyes kept clinging to each other every few seconds.

Oh yes, she was happy for her sister. But that still did not stop Saloni from feeling a touch of envy. No, envy was too mild a feeling. What she felt was way more than that. Saloni felt green with jealousy. Forget about holding hands, Manish never even looked her way, not with love anyway.

The women ordered cocktails; Manish asked for whisky and soda while Lakshman stuck to a single pint of beer. "You can't do that, man. We're celebrating your wedding. Come on Laki, have something stronger," implored Manish.

Lakshman smiled, shaking his head. "Let's not forget that I'm driving us back home."

"So who cares?" said Manish, at his sarcastic best. "I'm sure we can pull the wool over the policemen's eyes, what with two women in the car along with us."

Lakshman grinned. "That's not the point, is it? I don't need a policeman to keep me in order. Drunken driving is unsafe. And well, I don't much care for hard drinks anyway."

"Oh!" Manish nodded his head, not bothering to hide his sarcasm when he said, "You mean you can't hold your drink." He lifted his glass of whisky and downed it in one go, asking the waiter to bring him another.

Lakshman shrugged, refusing to rise to the bait, turning to look at his wife when she placed her head on his shoulder. "Tired?" he asked tenderly.

Ruma looked deeply into her husband's black gaze and said softly, obviously only for his ears, "Not really, just wanted to cuddle."

Saloni turned away to study the ambience of the restaurant when she noticed Lakshman's left arm snaking around Ruma's waist. And yes, she could not help overhearing Ruma's whispered words. She could not wait for dinner to be over and got up the moment she saw that everyone had finished with their meals. "Would you all mind if we leave now?" She was sure that the newly married couple must be eager to get back home too and she did not really care what her husband thought.

Lakshman got up from his chair immediately, saying, "Not at all. You must want to get back to little

Mitesh. I must say he's adorable." He smiled at his sister-in-law.

"*Arre yaar*, do sit down a bit longer. I want to have another drink," said Manish, his voice slurred as he had already had three large pegs by now. "And Mitesh should be fine. Saloni worries unnecessarily." He turned to give his wife a mocking look, not caring that he only hurt her more and more.

Lakshman sat back out of sheer politeness, his face expressionless now as he looked from Manish to Saloni, not saying anything, while he held Ruma's hand tightly against his thigh. The three of them waited for Manish to down his fourth drink and got up the moment he was done. Lakshman had already paid the bill, eager to leave, as were the two women.

Manish continued to lecture about his life in Chicago during their ride back home, while the other three remained silent.

Saloni felt like a voyeur as she could not help noticing the closeness between Ruma and Lakshman from her peripheral even though she did her best to keep her eyes glued to the window.

It was time she took charge of her life. Saloni hated being second best. And she seriously needed to rethink her life. Straightening her shoulders as she stepped out of the car, she decided that she would give Manish one final chance, to be a good—if not great—husband. Or... well, time would tell. She was not going to let him trample all over her. Sticking to her decision, Saloni preponed her return ticket to Chicago and left on the same flight as her husband, a week later.

itesh never appeared to stop complaining these days. The cheerful baby seemed to be picking up on his mother's irritated vibes and was cranky most of the time. Well, neither mother nor son was happy to be back in Chicago as they missed their big family back home.

Life was lonely now that it was just the two of them again, with Manish remaining busy, either at work or with his friends. He got back from work and invariably went out, every evening. "Leave my dinner on the table. I'll help myself," instructed Manish, pulling on his socks. He had changed out of his work clothes into a pair of jeans and a t-shirt, obviously planning to go pub hopping.

"Can't you stay home with us today?" asked Saloni, her eyes bleak.

"And do what? Watch TV? Forget it, Saloni. I'll be bored to death," he said, tying the laces of his sneakers.

"I'm sure Mitesh will love your company."

Manish turned to give her a sarcastic smile. "Do you really expect me to hold a conversation with a seven-month-old? Don't be stupid, Saloni. That's a mother's job. Bye." He left, without waiting to hear her reply.

A sudden memory triggered off in her head—of Aarav nine years ago and of the same man at Ruma's wedding. Missed opportunities! Saloni's lips drooped. *No*! She will not think about Aarav Chopra.

Saloni went to the sink to splash cold water on her face, also holding her wrists under the tap. She needed to cool down or she might smash something—maybe the ceramic figurines which filled the showcase in the drawing room. While it would have helped her let off steam by smashing every single piece of crockery in the house, she did not want to upset her little son.

If Manish wanted to spend all his free time with his friends, why the hell had he got married in the first place? She knew the answer, of course. House helps costed a lot of money in the USA. Cooks, even more. It was cheaper—no, smart business tactics, actually—to get married to a stupid woman from India who would do the cooking and cleaning for free, *after* bringing a hefty dowry to her NRI husband. And the man continued to lead a luxurious life. Imagine, the wife also kept his bed warm, available whenever *he* wanted to have sex.

This needed to stop, right now! Saloni straightened her shoulders. It was time to take charge of her life. Removing the phone from her skirt pocket, she called Pritesh, a close friend of Manish's. Of all her husband's friends, Pritesh was the only one who chose to speak to Saloni, beyond saying 'hi'. She made a plan with Pritesh to have a get together at her home on the coming Saturday.

"That would be awesome, Saloni. I have been wondering about you and that little son of yours. You both must be pretty lonely all by yourselves at home. A party at your apartment is such a great idea. I'll get the drinks. Let me see if anyone else is ready to pitch with a few other items so that you don't have to cook for the whole lot of us."

Pritesh's enthusiasm warmed Saloni's heart. "Shall I make *chicken biryani* and *raita*? It would be great if you could organise some snacks."

"Definitely! Let's have a ball. Do you have dance music? Or I can get some on a pen drive."

"I have all the music you want. No worries," said Saloni, a smile in her voice. She was desperate to meet people and could not wait for Saturday. "Alright then, Pritesh. Thanks. I'll see you on Saturday."

If Pritesh thought it strange that it was Saloni who was planning the party and not Manish, he did not say anything about it.

The party on Saturday was a super hit, by anyone's standards. There were thirty people in all and everyone appeared to have a great time, dancing, drinking and snacking on *pizza* slices and *samosas*. Each one of them complimented Saloni's choice of music and the *chicken biryani* which she had prepared. Manish's friends even chatted with Mitesh who was at his happiest from the time they had returned home.

It was 2 am when Saloni shut the door on the last guest and turned towards her silent husband with a wide smile on her face. "Wasn't that just lovely?!"

Manish walked towards her and stood in front of her, his stance threatening. "That's the last time you are organising a party behind my back. Do you hear me?" His voice was a feral growl.

Saloni blanched in shock. "Manish, I didn't plan anything behind your back. It was a surprise for you. I thought..."

"I hate surprises. And I don't give a damn about your reasons. Never do it to me again, do you hear?" His hands were clenched into fists, his face red with temper.

"But..."

"Shut up and listen to me Saloni. No inviting anyone into my house without my permission. And that should be clear to even the biggest idiot on earth." He did an about turn and went into his bedroom, slamming the door behind him, not caring that the sleeping infant woke up with a jerk and began to wail loudly.

But what did it matter to him? thought Saloni bitterly. Manish had moved into a separate bedroom when Mitesh had been barely a month old. He did not want his sleep disturbed. She rocked Mitesh back to sleep, feeding him from his bottle.

So it was his—Manish's—house. Saloni was beyond furious. She felt violent and needed to do something about it before she burst a blood vessel. Mindful of the baby sleeping in his cot, Saloni deliberately opened her wardrobe and brought out her wedding sari. The silk sari in red and brocade appeared to mock her. Taking out a pair of scissors, Saloni snipped the sari along the edge at various points before tearing it into shreds with her bare hands, throwing the strips on the floor and stamping all over them.

Phew!

She was finally calm, at least calmer than what she had been an hour ago. She would talk to Manish in the morning, appealing to his sense of logic, if he had one, that is. She simply had to get busy and interact with more people if she wanted to retain her sanity. But it looked as if she could do nothing without his permission.

Saloni took long and deep breaths. Losing her temper was not the answer. She would have that talk tomorrow, she thought decidedly before going to bed.

Manish had already left the house when Saloni woke up at eight in the morning.

Mumbai

It was seven in the evening when Akshay Malhotra, Shyam Malhotra's cousin and Saloni's *chachu*, sat down to an early dinner with his family. His father, Raj Malhotra, sat at the head of the table flanked by his grandchildren, seven-year-old Akshara on his left and four-year-old Suryansh on his right. Akshay's mother, Tanuja, sat next to Akshara while Akshay took the chair beside Suryansh. His wife, Sunita, helped the cook bring all the dishes to the table before she settled in the chair next to Akshay's.

"Okay, my grandchildren and I have a plan," said Raj with a mischievous grin on his face as he took a piece of *roti* and dipped it into the chicken gravy before popping it into his mouth.

Akshara giggled, staring adoringly at her grandfather, even as she held her grandmother's hand tightly, seething with excitement.

Tanuja laughed when Suryansh gurgled too, giving his parents a corner-eyed glance before turning to wink at his grandfather.

"What?" asked Akshay, placing the spoon back on his plate, "What are you guys cooking up? Mom, do you know? Sunita?" He turned to both women in turn, dragging out the suspense as the kids seemed so thrilled about it.

Tanuja continued to grin, shaking her head while Sunita shrugged, saying, "I don't know. What's the plan, Dad?"

Raj grinned at the kids in turn and asked, "Should I tell them?"

"Yes please, Dada," chorused Akshara and Suryansh.

"Akshay, Sunita, I've booked tickets and a hotel suite for your stay in London for four days..."

"What?" Akshay gave his father a startled look, though amused. "You're sending just the two of us..."

Tanuja nodded. "You see, we're letting you both go by yourselves for some time, only because the four of us are going on a special kiddies' holiday after your trip so that you don't insist on going along with us." Her eyes glinted with mischief.

"Yes," said Suryansh. "Mummy and Daddy can't go with us to... we aren't telling them now, are we Dada?" He turned to ask his grandfather.

"Of course, we aren't," said Raj, shaking his head, "That's our secret. So, you guys are leaving tomorrow."

Sunita laughed, getting up to hug Raj. "Thank you, Dad! You're the best." She walked to Tanuja and gave her a hug too. "Mom, are you sure you can manage?" she asked her in a whisper.

"Of course we can, princess." Tanuja hugged her daughter-in-law right back. "It has been a long time since Akshay and you had a holiday by yourselves."

Sunita was truly touched by her parents-in-laws' gesture as she sat next to Akshay, holding his hand, too choked to do justice to her meal. She was thoroughly excited at the idea of spending some private time with her handsome husband whom she adored like crazy. She excused herself immediately after the meal to pack their bags. They were flying by British Airways the next afternoon, directly to Heathrow airport. Sunita took barely half an hour to complete her packing and rushed back downstairs where Suryansh and Akshara were taking turns reading a fairy tale aloud, to Tanuja and Raj. This was a daily post-dinner ritual which neither the grandparents nor the grandchildren wanted to miss. With a smile on her face, Sunita went to sit next to Akshay who was still working on his laptop.

"All set?" he asked her softly, his dark brown eyes gazing into her grey-green ones in adoration.

Sunita nodded, her eyes glowing with excitement. "Am I being very selfish wanting to take off with only you?" She expressed the fleeting moment of guilt to her husband of nine years.

"Nope. I'm sure we'll return all rejuvenated to become even better parents to our children, don't you think?"

"I suppose. Anyway, I think the four of them," she pointed towards the quartet huddled around the centre table, "are absolutely fine with it."

"Exactly. Do you need to complete anything urgent?" Akshay asked his interior designer wife. "I'm just dashing off a few mails and plan to leave my laptop back at home. I might even use a separate SIM on my phone so that only the family can reach us," said Akshay.

"I don't have anything urgent lined up. Mom knows that, which is probably the reason why they decided to surprise us right at this moment. I'll let you get on with your work then. I'm off to soak in the bathtub and get myself all ready for our holiday," said Sunita, getting up from the chair next to him.

"Hey!" Akshay turned from his laptop to look up at his gorgeous wife, "Do you want to wait until the kids get to sleep? I can join you." He closed his left eye in a slow wink, a grin splitting his attractive features.

Sunita gave him an answering grin even as her cheeks bloomed fierily, despite all these years of being married to Akshay. "It's a date."

The next four days were pure bliss as they strolled around London during the day, checking out the many sights, while making long and leisurely love through the nights.

"Akshay." Sunita turned her head sideways to give him better access as he nibbled her earlobe. They were leaving the next evening to go back home.

"Sweetheart," he whispered, his tongue tracing the outline of her ear, arousing her yet again.

She turned to kiss the corner of his mouth, her tongue reaching to trace over the seam of his lips. And the ritual began yet again as they made love, reaching out to the zenith once more.

Akshay sat up with a jerk when his phone rang loudly. He lifted it to notice with surprise that it was his niece Saloni from Chicago.

"Hey Saloni! How have you been?" asked Akshay, turning to look at his wife to see if she realised who was on the phone. Sunita nodded her head in understanding, her hand holding Akshay's between both of her own.

"Not good, Akshay *Chachu*." Saloni's voice was gruff, disturbing him badly along with her words.

"What happened *beta*?" The *'beta'* slipped out automatically as he realised that Saloni probably needed a lot of reassurance. She was barely a decade younger to him.

"I want to get back to Delhi along with Mitesh; and I need to buy tickets. Can you help me?"

OMG! What must have happened for Saloni to take this sudden decision? She had returned to Chicago barely a couple of months ago.

"Do you want to talk about it?" suggested Akshay cautiously, putting the call on speaker mode so that Sunita could also hear. "Sunita's with me, Saloni. And my phone's on speaker now."

"Okay, though I don't want to talk about it right now. Sorry about that Sunita." Sunita was barely a couple of years older than Saloni and preferred to be addressed by only her name without the tag of *chachi*. "It's just that I want to catch the first flight out. I can't live with Manish any longer. He has no respect for me as a human being, let alone a woman. He doesn't give a damn about our son either. I hate it out here. I'm sorry to trouble you..."

"What's this, Saloni? Family's no trouble at all. But..."

"I can't afford to buy our flight tickets. Can you help me?" It was obvious that Saloni was desperate even though she strived hard to keep her voice as neutral as possible.

"Of course, I can help you, Saloni. But will you be able to travel alone with Mitesh?" Akshay was getting worried now. The toddler was going to be eight months, a difficult age to be cooped up during a long flight. And Mitesh had travelled both ways a little less than a couple of months ago.

Sunita had already logged into her phone to check out flights from Chicago to London. "There's a flight from Chicago at 7.20 pm today local time. It will reach London at 9.05 tomorrow morning," she said.

Akshay gave his wife a thumbs-up before addressing Saloni. "Sunita and I are in London. You come over with Mitesh and we'll travel together to India. Is that alright with you?"

"*Chachu!*" Saloni's voice broke. They could hear her sniffling as she paused, obviously struggling to get her voice back in control. "Thank you. And Sunita, you too. I'm leaving right now, before Manish gets back from work."

"But Saloni, what if he gets worried? I hope you're going to leave him a message." That was Sunita.

"Of course I plan to do that. Bye, guys. I'll see you in the morning. Akshay *Chachu*, please don't bother to come to the airport. Just send me the tickets and your hotel address on WhatsApp. I'm travelling light, with only a backpack."

"Okay dear. You take care and have a safe flight," said Akshay before disconnecting. Sunita had already booked the tickets for one adult and an infant and messaged Saloni. "Damn the guy. I always thought Manish was cold-blooded and too full of Chicago," muttered Akshay. "But Rati *bhabhi* was so insistent on getting them married. Tch! Poor Saloni. A more level-headed girl I'm yet to see. And she did so well in her studies too. It was so bloody unfair to uproot her from Delhi and move her to the USA where she can't do a damn thing but twiddle her thumbs."

Sunita hugged her husband close, not saying anything. It was rare for the cheerful Akshay to rant about anything; which just went to show how upset he was.

Saloni left home ten minutes later, Mitesh in his collapsible pram and a backpack on her shoulders with one change of clothes for herself, a few sets of clothes, disposable nappies and eight bottles of feed for her son. She checked that she had some cash and their passports in her bag before leaving the apartment's keys on the hall table, weighing down the brief note which she had written to him. She got into the cab she had called for and left without turning to look back at the apartment block which held some of the unhappiest moments of her life in the last two-plus years.

As she was leaving, Saloni promised herself that she was not returning to this place ever, come hell or high water. Her mother could throw all the tantrums she wanted. From now on, she would answer to no one and remain her own boss.

8

Aarav did his best to concentrate on the meeting he had called with all his heads of departments. But it was difficult as he kept looking at the picture Saloni's husband had sent on his WhatsApp that morning. While the man had chopped Saloni out of the picture when he had posted it on Twitter, he had sent the original picture to Aarav. Saloni was standing next to him, her hand on his forearm while Aarav held little Mitesh in the crook of his arm. It was a darling picture and made Aarav emotional every time he looked at it. Why Manish had chosen to send the unedited version after all this long was anyone's guess.

Aarav looked up from his phone when there was a lull. "I'm sorry. Charmaine, you were saying...?"

His accounts department head looked at her boss, wondering if something was the matter. Aarav usually showed a lot of enthusiasm and kept the meetings going, so much so that his staff looked forward to getting together with him as often as they could as they felt energised every time they were done with one. "Aren't you keeping well, Aarav?" Charmaine asked him outright.

Aarav shook his head, appearing rather sheepish. "I'm sorry, just a bit distracted." He raised his hands in front of him in a gesture of defence. "No excuse. Carry on guys. So, what do you think? Should we take up this mega wedding project? As you all know, we have been into corporate events as well as movie and TV awards. If we take this on, we'll be deviating from our regular line. But," he paused for effect, "It's a whole new challenge with lots of learning for all of us. This is a destination wedding with a no-holds-barred budget." He paused for effect before saying, "Now shoot!"

Dharmesh, the head of HR, said, "I vote for it. This could be huge, especially considering who the clients are." The clients were an old family from a royal line from Mysore. They still lived in a palace on the outskirts of the city and owned five hundred acres of flourishing land.

Vinaya, from the art department, said, "I'm totally excited, my head already buzzing with ideas. What if we have the wedding on a cruise ship—with the whole works? It could be over four days or even seven."

Aarav laughed, showing a thumbs-up before turning to Charmaine who said, a wide grin on her face, "I'm all for it. You did say the budget is unlimited, right?"

The other three department heads were also in, though Ganesh from marketing had some questions.

"Recently, our clients have given us *carte blanche* on their projects. Since this is a family thing, they might have a lot of conditions. Shouldn't we find out what they have to say before committing ourselves? At no point can we fail to deliver."

"That's a valid point, Ganesh," said Aarav, making a note on a scribble pad. "I'm having a preliminary meeting with them, at their palace..." He paused when the others 'ooh'ed and 'aah'ed, before continuing, "Next week. The wedding date is some six months from now. Let me find out all their requirements. Hiten, we'll be travelling on Tuesday and probably stay back until Thursday evening. Ask Deepak to keep himself free during that time until the end of the week. We'll leave for Mysore at 8 am on Tuesday. Let's keep the return date open. It'll depend on how the meetings go." Deepak Sinhal was the pilot who flew the private twenty-seater jet that Aarav owned.

Hiten, Aarav's executive assistant, said, "Consider it done Aarav," as he made a note on his phone.

"That's about it for now. Anyone has anything else to say?" When there were no questions from his excited staff, Aarav smiled and concluded the meeting. "Right then, we'll meet again tentatively on Friday next in this regard."

Aarav slumped back in his chair when everyone left, opening his phone once again to look at the picture of Saloni and her son. He straightened after a few seconds, shaking off the feeling of melancholy. It did not make sense, pining for her. Saloni was taken. Well, he could not stop loving her, but that did not mean he needed to be sad about it. Wishing the mother and child all happiness—no, he refused to include her husband in his wishes—Aarav got up to leave his cabin and join the rest of his staff for lunch.

9

kshay and Sunita met Saloni at Heathrow despite her protests. They took her back to the hotel where they had booked a room for her. Sunita took charge of Mitesh, insisting that Saloni needed to sleep. "We are flying in barely another ten hours, Saloni. It's best you get some rest. Let me take care of Mitesh."

Saloni hugged Sunita tightly, not saying a word as the latter left her alone, carrying Mitesh along with her. It was 5 am in Chicago and she was totally beat. Was she glad there was someone to care for Mitesh!

Lying on the bed, Saloni shut her eyes, only to see Manish behind her closed eyes, the way he had behaved that morning before leaving for work.

Saloni had overslept by half an hour and had not been able to get a hot breakfast ready for him. All she had had to offer were cornflakes and milk along with fresh coffee. And this was the first time she had not prepared something fresh for him in the morning.

"If it's cornflakes that I wanted to eat, why the hell did I get married to you?" Manish asked her, his eyes red with temper. "What the hell do you do all day long? Watch TV and gossip over the phone, right? Couldn't you get up a bit early and prepare something edible for your husband who slogs all day at work?"

"I'm sorry Manish. You know I've never done this before. It's just that..."

"Just what? You're useless in bed. Now you don't want to do anything in the kitchen. Give me one reason why you should continue to be my wife." He finished his coffee and left with the parting shot, "I need to speak to my mom. She'd better know how wrong she had been in choosing you for my wife."

Is it I or he who is useless in bed? Saloni fumed in absolute disgust. Was there any use asking him the question? Before she became pregnant, Manish had chosen to bed her on an average of once a week, when he felt like it. The few times she had approached him, he had accused her of disturbing his sleep and had even called her a 'nymphomaniac' a couple of times. Saloni had shrunk within herself, beginning to believe his words. Maybe women weren't supposed to feel the need for sex. But somehow, deep down, she did not quite believe that. But there was no one she could discuss the matter with.

But today, Manish had crossed an invisible line of decency. He had accused Saloni of being useless in bed, when he had stopped allowing her in it after Mitesh's birth. And this was the first time she had not given him a hot breakfast since their marriage. How unfair was this?!

Saloni straightened up. This was it. She had given their marriage her best. She had gone against her instincts to return to Chicago with Manish, cutting short her holiday in Delhi. And what had she got in return? Forget about being loved, Manish treated her like dirt.

And whose fault was that? It was no use blaming Manish. He was what he was, a spoilt brat of a patriarchal family. He obviously thought that women had been created by God to serve the likes of him. But if Saloni continued to cater to his whims, then she would be the one who would be at fault, making him believe that he was absolutely right.

This was not going to work. It was obvious that Manish cared only about himself and not for his wife and their child. No, Mitesh was *her* baby—only hers. She could not recall a single time when the child's biological father had lifted him in his arms.

A scene inadvertently flashed before her eyes—of Mitesh in Aarav's arms. Saloni smiled despite her sadness. That just went to prove that all men weren't bad. The present situation she found herself in, was all thanks to her mother Rati. Her ambitious mother had been hell bent on making a high society match for her eldest born and had managed to pick up a piece of coal, giving a miss to the diamond in the vicinity. Saloni laughed, despite herself, at the irony of that.

But first things first! Saloni wondered how she could get out of her marriage. She quickly prepared breakfast and lunch for herself and fed Mitesh. "Would you like to go to Delhi sweetheart? I'm sure we both will be happier there. What say?" she asked him, as he held his feeding bottle with both his hands, his tiny legs up in the air.

Mitesh stopped feeding to give his mother a brilliant smile as if he understood what she had said.

"You agree? So Delhi it is, little guy. We both will have a wonderful life there." She bent down to kiss the infant on his forehead before placing him inside his playpen. He had been doing his best to sit nowadays.

Saloni checked the cost of flights from Chicago to Delhi. There were no direct flights that day and they all seemed to take more than forty hours. She checked some more, wondering if she could travel to either Amsterdam or London and catch a connecting flight from there. But would she be able to manage the trip with a toddler?

She had one credit card, with a limit of fifty thousand rupees which she could use from here. That would not be sufficient to buy their tickets. What to do?

If she contacted her father, he would immediately discuss it with her mother. And Rati would kill Saloni first before trying to find out why her daughter was keen to leave her husband and return home to her parents.

Ruma? No, her sister was newly married and was obviously having a wonderful life. It was not fair to burden her with her problems, not right now.

Saloni snapped her fingers when Akshay *Chachu* came to mind. Her father's young cousin from Mumbai was a rock-solid man. He was the best person one could turn to in time of trouble. Saloni could not help the smile which came to her lips when she thought of the way he had stood in support along with her grandma when Ruma had married Lakshman in secret. The smile disappeared even as a deep sigh shuddered through her being. Maybe, just maybe, she should have spoken to her grandmother Ganga when her marriage was being fixed with Manish. Well, her mother had not given her a choice. After meeting Manish and not seeing anything to fault with him, Saloni had gone along with the tide. Only, she had not expected to be stranded in the middle of the ocean. And her marriage had not been one hundred percent bad. It had given her little Mitesh and that was one thing Saloni could never regret.

So, it had to be Akshay *Chachu* to the rescue. It was almost four in the evening when she finally got through to him, after his mother, Saloni's great aunt Tanuja, gave her the alternate number which he was using during his holiday. By then she had already packed all the stuff she required for her trip back home to India.

God bless both, Akshay *Chachu* and his wife Sunita. They had not asked too many questions and luckily, they were both in London, ready to escort her back home. Saloni only needed to manage the trip from Chicago to London on her own and then she would be safe with her family. The thought helped ease her restlessness a little.

Her mind in a turmoil with all these thoughts about the past dogging it, Saloni did not know when she slipped into a deep sleep in the hotel room in London, more at peace than she had been in a long time.

When the four of them—Akshay, Sunita, Saloni, and Mitesh—reached Mumbai, Raj had already left for Singapore with Tanuja and the kids. Akshay had decided to take Saloni to his home in Mumbai first. Sunita was also in agreement. While Saloni had not shed a single tear, it was obvious that the younger woman's confidence was shaken terribly.

"Saloni, let's first have a skype chat with Ganga *Chachi*. What say?" He had already called the Malhotra matriarch and spoken to her briefly about the situation.

"Okay," said Saloni. "Do you think we can do it privately, only with her? I don't want Mamma to be a part of it. I..."

Akshay nodded. "But of course. You don't worry about that. We'll talk to your grandma once she's retired to her room."

"Thank you so much, Akshay *Chachu*. I don't really know how I would have managed without you and Sunita..." Saloni stopped speaking when her voice choked with the emotion clogging her throat.

"Shut up Saloni," said Akshay, hugging her. "Don't keep thanking us again and again. We Malhotras stand up for each other, don't we?"

Saloni nodded, biting her lip hard to stop herself from crying. She was not a coward. It was just that she was petrified of facing her mother. But then, she could not just pile up on Akshay and Sunita forever. She moved away to rub her hands over her face, straightening her shoulders and giving Akshay a small smile. "*Chalo*, let's talk to *Daadima*."

Akshay set up his laptop in the guest bedroom and while connecting Saloni to her grandmother, said, "You go ahead and have your chat, Saloni. I'm going to play with your little guy." He left, closing the door behind him.

"*Daadima*..." Saloni broke down as soon as she saw her darling grandmother's face on the laptop screen.

"Saloni *beta*, what has Manish done to you?" Ganga frowned fiercely from the screen. "Did he dare to beat you?"

Laughing through her tears, Saloni shook her head. "No *Daadima*. He wouldn't dare, unless he wanted his arm broken."

Ganga smiled, her frown disappearing. "That's my girl. So tell me. Does he know that you have left him? And that's what you've done, right?"

"He should know by now, I'm sure. I left him a note. I know I should have called and told him or at least sent him a WhatsApp message, but *Daadima*, he doesn't deserve any courtesy, believe me. And yes, I have left him." Saloni valiantly squared her drooping shoulders once again. "And I don't plan to go back, *Daadima*, whatever Mamma says. If all she wanted for me was the life of an unpaid servant—no, not a servant, but a slave—then why did she get me educated? I..." And with that, the floodgates opened. Saloni poured her heart out to her grandmother, as she regaled her with incident after incident of all the pain and ego battering which she had undergone at her husband's hands from the beginning of her marriage.

"He does not even like me, *Daadima*. He has told me a number of times that I'm too fat to be a suitable partner in bed. We have not made love..." Saloni broke off. Well, it was best that *Daadima* knew everything, "From the time Mitesh was born. It looks like he wants me there only to cook his meals and clean his house. This wasn't how I had envisaged my life."

"Oh my God!" *Daadima* had never thought very highly of Manish, though she had kept her opinion to herself. But even she had not expected it to be this bad. "Didn't you try getting a job, *beta*? I love little Mitesh too. But don't you think a job would have made you more independent?"

"Do you think I didn't try? My visa doesn't allow it. I even asked Manish if we could shift back to Delhi. But then, he thinks the earth revolves around Chicago. And *Daadima*, he's interested in neither Mitesh nor me. Will you believe me if I tell you that he hasn't held the baby in his arms even once?"

"The bastard!" Ganga had no trouble calling Manish names. She had a fierce sense of independence and adored all her grandchildren. Just now, she felt sorry that she had not interfered when her daughter-in-law Rati had fixed Saloni's wedding within two days of her getting her MBA results. That the child had come first in the university had never counted with her mother. "Saloni, I'm coming over to Mumbai and will bring you back home to Delhi. Let me see who stops you."

Saloni smiled at her grandmother, hope fluttering in her heart. "*Daadima*, have I ever told you how much I love you?"

Three days later, Ganga Malhotra walked into the Malhotra residence in Delhi with her granddaughter and great grandson in tow. Just like she had expected, within five minutes of their arrival, all hell broke loose.

11

Ganga and Akshay had got their heads together and planned Saloni's arrival in Delhi to coincide with her father and brothers being present at home. They arrived just before dinner exactly when Vinayak, the cook, was placing the food on the dining table.

"Saloni *beta*, this is a surprise," said Shyam, getting up from his chair to give his daughter a hug before lifting his grandson into his arms. "You have become so big, young man," he told the chortling baby who was happy to be among so many familiar faces.

Saloni's eyes went in search of her mother even as she returned her father's hug, unable to curb the flash of fear which sprang up despite all of Ganga's reassurances.

Rati dropped the holder containing the spoons and forks with a clang even as her eyes went wide in shock. "Saloni..." Her voice was a raw whisper before she gathered her wits together and strode in a rush across the living room towards her eldest born. "What the hell are you doing here? Is Manish with you?" Her words were a shriek now even as her gaze pierced her daughter's, like a laser beam.

"No Mamma." Saloni tucked her hands into her jeans' pockets so that her mother would not notice their trembling. "He has not come. It is only Mitesh and I."

"But you just went back to your home." Rati scowled fiercely at her daughter.

"Rati, let us all have dinner first. Saloni must also be hungry. We can talk later," said Shyam, striving for peace as always.

"Yeah Mom, let's eat before everything turns cold," said Shaan, the youngest of the siblings—Saloni, Ruma, Ryan and Shaan, in that order.

Ryan ignored all of them as he held his little nephew in his arms, making monkey faces at the little boy who chortled at his young uncle's antics.

Rati turned away angrily to walk to the table. She did not speak with anyone as she ate her meal without tasting it.

Vinayak took Mitesh from Ryan's arms. "You have your dinner, Ryan. I'll take care of Mitesh *baba*." The love was mutual as Mitesh pulled at Vinayak's black and white moustache, laughing as if he had met an old friend.

Saloni also remained silent as the other four chatted desultorily about this and that. Her throat clogged up as she tried to eat and she gave up after a few bites.

Rati pushed her plate away and got up. "Now tell me, what are you doing here? A wife's place is with her husband. Haven't I taught you that?"

Saloni gave her grandmother and father a pathetic look before facing her mother, giving a small nod.

"So?"

"I don't want to live with Manish any more, Mamma." Saloni dropped her bombshell. Well, there was no other way to say it.

Ryan and Shaan had also finished eating by now and were listening avidly. Shyam gave his daughter a startled look. Though he never said much, thanks to his hyper wife, Shyam was extremely observant. He had noticed that everything was not well with Saloni's life when she had come down for Ruma's wedding. But to leave her husband?! Something terrible must have happened. He knew that his daughter was pretty level headed.

"What?!" Rati shrieked at the top of her voice. "Are you mad, girl? How can you treat your husband like a set of clothes or a pair of footwear—use one day and discard the next?"

"But Mamma, you don't know what happened. I..."

"So tell me *na*? I'm all ears." The tempest in Rati's gaze would have shrivelled a lesser person.

Shyam went to his daughter and hugged her before seating her next to him on a sofa. "Rati, will you please calm down? Saloni is obviously upset. Let her..."

"So? Can't you see that I am upset that my daughter has left her husband after barely two years of marriage? Here I thought that I was done with all my responsibilities as both my daughters were settled with excellent husbands and one returns even before I have taken a deep breath." Rati glared at her husband before turning to her daughter. "How can you do this to me, Saloni?" Tears ran down her cheeks.

Saloni gave her mother a bitter look, wondering how she always managed to turn the tears on and off at will. "Mamma, Manish doesn't care for me. He doesn't want a wife, but a servant. I..."

Rati gave a bitter laugh. "But isn't that the role of wives? I also work like a servant here in this house..."

"Mamma, don't be ridiculous," said Ryan, looking deeply at his mother. "You live like a queen. Pappa listens to everything you say."

Ganga raised the edge of her sari to cover her grinning lips. That was a good shot from unexpected quarters.

If looks could kill, Ryan would have dropped dead by now. "Shut up Ryan, you are a kid, you don't know anything," shouted Rati before turning to glare at Saloni again. Luckily for her, she did not notice the humour in her mother-in-law's eyes or her temper might have hit the roof.

"Oh yeah, at twenty going on twenty-one, I would be treated like a kid only in India." Ryan did not bother to hide his sarcasm.

"Ryan, go away, will you? You are distracting us." Rati yelled once again at her son before pinning Saloni with her sharp gaze. "So tell me, what is wrong in doing honest housework? You..."

"If it is housework that you wanted me to do, why the hell was I sent to university? To complete my MBA at that?" Saloni did not yell, though she badly wanted to.

"Exactly my point." Rati's voice was triumphant as she turned her accusing gaze to her husband. "*Kyunji*, you answer her question. Why the hell did we educate her?"

Ganga entered the conversation, not giving her son a chance to respond. "We educated Saloni to empower her, to help her stand on her own feet, to make sure that she doesn't become dependent on another person, whether it is her father, husband or son." She, for one, had never approved of Rati remaining a housewife. There were enough servants to take care of the house. As an educated woman, Rati should have taken up a career. With no work for her brain, she had channelled all her energy into finding grooms for her girls. In a few years' time, she would go in search of brides for her sons. What else was there to do?

"And see the result of all that empowerment. Saloni has turned out to be an egotist. She refuses to live with her husband who is a decent..."

"Stop it, Rati." Ganga's voice rose.

Rati's jaw fell wide open as she gave her mother-in-law a shocked look. She had never, but never, heard the matriarch raise her voice.

"You haven't even bothered to find out why your intelligent daughter has chosen to leave her husband while you insist on burying your head in the sand. If Saloni has run away, all the way from Chicago to Delhi, with a babe-in-arms, there should be a valid reason, right? Shouldn't you try to find out what that is, instead of shouting at her? A parent's duty is to make sure that her child has a good life. A parent's *love* ensures that she has a happy life. Just getting Saloni married isn't enough; at least, not for me."

When Ganga paused to take a much-needed breath, Shyam spoke. "Saloni, if you think that Manish is unfit to be your husband, I believe you. I trust your judgement. This has never stopped being your home. You are welcome to stay here along with Mitesh until I am alive. I will ensure that you have a flat in your own name after I'm gone." He got up, indicating that the matter was closed, pulling his daughter into his arms in a fierce hug. Ryan went forward and hugged his sister too, welcoming her back into the fold.

Ganga wiped her streaming eyes, proud of her son. Shyam rarely spoke against his wife's shenanigans, but his heart was obviously in the right place.

While Rati stood there fuming with temper while tears threatened to fall from her eyes, Shaan, her youngest, gave her a fierce hug. "Take a chill pill, Mom. You need to loosen up."

"Don't be silly, Shaan. How can I? Marriage is such a serious business." Rati gave her youngest born a stern look.

"Yes Mom. I don't deny that," he smiled at her. "But Sal's happiness is way more important, isn't it? Do you want her to live a sad life over the next half a century until "death does them part"? He drew quotation marks in the air, a cheeky expression on his face.

"*Yeh* Mom Mom *kya laga rakka hai?* Mamma *bolo.*" Rati's glare turned fiercer.

Shaan laughed, hugging her tighter. "Sure Mom."

12

Manish went home at seven that evening to find the house empty. Not too bothered when he did not find Saloni and Mitesh at home, he had a shower and changed into fresh clothes before leaving the apartment to meet a few friends. He sent Saloni a WhatsApp message saying, "You haven't made food today at all it seems. Come back home immediately and make some hot *rotis* and my favourite *fish curry*. I should be home by eleven."

He did not bother to check if the message had reached her phone or whether she had read it, confident that his wife must be cowed down enough to do his bidding after the scolding he had given her in the morning. He was glad to be out, unwinding after a hard day at the hospital. He chatted non-stop, downing two pints of beer, munching on a slice of pizza. When his friends insisted on more, he refused with an unmasked glee. "My wife must have prepared my favourite dinner for me and I don't want to miss it," he grinned. He loved to show off to his friends of the wonderful way his wife took care of him, feeding him the best meals. It felt good to know that they felt envious, not that any of them had mentioned feeling that way. But then, what anybody else thought never really concerned Manish. He got down from his bar stool at half past ten and left, bidding his friends goodnight.

Entering his flat at exactly eleven, Manish was eager to have his favourite meal. What greeted him, however, was absolute silence. Was Mitesh unusually asleep? Where was Saloni?

"Saloni!" Manish called out a few times before walking around the two-bedroom apartment in search of her. He even checked the bathrooms, only to find them empty. What the hell!

He opened his phone to check if she was online and noticed that his message had never reached her phone. Had she lost her phone? Turning to the hall table, he noticed her keys. Grrr... the idiot had forgotten her keys. But she could have called him!

Manish angrily went closer when he noticed the yellow post-it which was placed under the key bunch. "I've left for Delhi. Goodbye!" She had not even bothered to sign the note.

What the fuck!

Manish's stomach growled, as if on cue. *What am I supposed to have for dinner now?* Which was the only thing Manish was bothered about.

He called his mother and spoke to her for half an hour, heaping all kind of abuses on Saloni's head. He also shouted at his mother for getting him married to a useless woman.

"I'll try to get a flight to Delhi as soon as I can. Her parents have a lot to answer for," growled Manish before disconnecting the call.

That he went to bed hungry did not cool his temper one bit. As he went on blaming Saloni for all *his suffering*, it never even struck him that he could have ordered for a home delivered meal.

Saloni moved into her old room where a baby cot was attached to her bed for Mitesh. Bindi was back in their employ, her position long term, this time round.

"Don't worry too much about your mother," Shyam whispered to his daughter on an aside, "Her bark is worse than her bite."

Saloni smiled at her father, absolutely touched by his support. He had not asked her anything about her life with Manish, taking only her word for it.

A couple of days later, the doorbell rang just as they were finishing breakfast. Ryan opened the door to admit Manish and his parents.

Shyam and Ganga went forward to greet them. "Please sit down," said Shyam. Turning towards the kitchen, he called out, "Vinayak, get some water and tea. Have you had breakfast?"

"We are not here to socialise." Manish's father, Parikshit Chawla, answered rudely. "We are here to give Saloni a second chance and allow her to redeem herself. Manish is ready to forgive her and take her back." Now he smiled magnanimously.

Saloni stood in the background, flanked by her younger, but tall and muscular brothers. Both Ryan and Shaan placed their hands protectively on her trembling shoulders, making her aware of their complete support.

Ganga raised a hand to stop Rati from saying anything when the latter stepped forward to speak to the Chawlas. "Manish is ready to forgive Saloni for what?" she asked in a stern voice. Ganga had a golden heart, but she was also a shrewd business woman who had a major role in running the family business.

"Huh?! For serving him cornflakes for breakfast, of course; and for running away scared. *Arre*, he is so young and works really hard. Alright, he has a bit of a temper. You advise your daughter not to mind all that and return home."

"Stop it, Dad. Who said I'm ready to forgive Saloni?" Manish gave his father a black look before turning to Shyam. "Uncle, I want you to ask your daughter why she is being so mean to me. What did I ever do to deserve this treatment? I have given her everything that a woman could want..."

"Everything? Are you sure about that, *beta*?" Ganga quirked an eyebrow up, her gaze sharp as she looked Manish up and down.

"You are insulting my son," snarled Anita, Manish's mother. "What do you mean by that question? I am keeping quiet with due respect to your age. But you cannot offend the son-in-law of your house."

"Has Manish told you everything?" Ganga turned her attention to Manish's mother. Shyam did not say anything as he was not aware of what had happened in Chicago.

"What is there to tell? A hardworking doctor needs to have a proper meal first thing in the morning. Saloni doesn't have any responsibility other than to take care of her husband. How could she serve him cornflakes? Which husband will keep quiet after that? Can you imagine a girl running away from home because of a bit of scolding?" Anita scowled, before turning to glare at Saloni. *"Bade ghar ki beti* we thought! We were sure she must be well brought up. But obviously not. I..."

Ganga raised a hand to stop the other woman from speaking further. "Is that what your son told you? That serving cornflakes for breakfast was the only issue? Do you really believe that my granddaughter would have left him for such a trivial thing?"

Anita looked down at the carpet, unable to meet the older woman's sharp gaze. Parikshit took up from there. "What else? My son is handsome, well educated, earning very well and lives in a posh apartment in Chicago. So many families were in queue to get their daughters married to him. We agreed to Saloni's match amidst all those. She should realise how lucky she is."

"You are right," piped up Rati, unable to control herself. "Saloni is indeed lucky to have a husband like Manish. I am sure she is sorry for..."

"I am not!" While Saloni's voice was barely a thread of a whisper, it was firm.

"What?!" Four voices asked the question simultaneously. Manish was on his feet as was Rati, while his parents continued to sit on the sofa, stunned at their daughter-in-law's words.

"I am not sorry. As Manish very well knows, it was not just the cornflakes." She appealed to her parents-in-law. "Ask your son if he has ever lifted Mitesh in his arms even once since he was born more than eight months ago. Ask him if he has touched me, his wife, even once in the same time. He..."

Parikshit also hung his head now, unable to face the accusations thrown against his son. Manish was beyond furious. Treating his wife like a doormat behind closed doors was one thing. The whole thing exposed to the world was another matter altogether.

"You should be ashamed to discuss our private life like this Saloni," he snarled, his voice ferocious.

"But why? Everyone here is family, right? What did you think? That I would be scared of talking about your behaviour openly and you could continue to walk all over me? Get yourself a servant, Manish. You don't need, no wait, actually you don't *deserve* a wife." She turned to her parents-in-law. "I mean no offence to you both, Uncle, Aunty. But I refuse to go back to live with Manish. And that is my final decision."

Saloni did an about turn and walked up the stairs to her room, taking her son along with her. She was glad that Manish's parents had shown no interest in meeting their grandson. Now that might have unsettled her.

Parikshit and Anita stood up. "We never expected to be insulted so badly. We'll send you the divorce papers at the earliest opportunity. Come along Manish, let's go."

Manish went, having no words to defend himself.

Rati continued to ignore her daughter in the coming days, too disturbed by the situation which had gone beyond her control. She also spoke very little to her husband and mother-in-law.

She could understand Ganga's behaviour. It was Shyam's attitude which shocked her. The man who listened to her, always, seemed to have changed overnight. It did not strike her that her peace-loving husband, who was generally easy going, falling with all her plans, could not stand back to watch his daughter leading an unhappy life. All these years, there had been no need for Shyam to go against his wife's wishes. She liked to rule the home front and he was perfectly fine with taking a back seat. This was the first time Shyam had refused to toe the line. And that had thrown Rati completely.

She refused to go to her weekly kitty party that Wednesday, too ashamed to face her friends. It looked like Rati's life was in shambles, all thanks to her rebellious daughter.

14

Ruma arrived a couple of hours after Manish and his family left. She entered Saloni's room and gave her sister a hug. "Are you okay, Sal?" She looked deep into her sister's eyes, trying to gauge the truth.

Saloni grinned at Ruma. "I feel awesome, Ruma." She rushed across and shut the door just in case their mother walked in suddenly. "I feel so free."

Ruma laughed. "I'm so glad to know that, Sal. Was a bit worried for you. What happened? Do you want to talk?"

The sisters chatted for a long time. There was a lot of laughter and some tears as Saloni narrated the story of her brief married life.

Ruma's lips drooped. "Are you saying that Manish has shown no interest in Mitesh at all? But how mean is that? Why the hell did he get married in the first place? Sal, I'm really sorry. I shouldn't have encouraged you to meet the man when Mamma suggested it. What a bastard! I..."

"Hey, don't be silly. There won't be a Mitesh if I hadn't married Manish. So, I'm not complaining."

Saloni smiled softly, thinking of her son who was downstairs in his playpen, having the time of his life with Ryan and Shaan, who were having a holiday.

Ruma nodded her head, saying, "I suppose. But Sal, you've been suffering so much and none of us had known anything about it. I wish I had spoken more to you. So stupid of me! I thought that you must be so busy as a newly married woman, setting up home with your hubby in a new place and all that, that I shouldn't disturb you too much. I..."

"Shall we stop this blame game?" Saloni grinned at her. "Right now, I'm just happy to have had a lucky escape. And I have you to thank for that, actually." When Ruma raised an enquiring eyebrow, she continued, "It was when I saw your closeness with Laki that it really struck me what I was missing. Forget about being touchy-feely or even PDA, Manish never wanted to make love."

Ruma turned red when she heard her sister. "I don't know what to say, Sal. I..."

"Why don't you congratulate me? Maybe you can buy me an exotic flower arrangement. We'll go out for a celebratory dinner, just you and me, like old times. What say? I'm serious."

Ruma stared at Saloni in awe as it slowly struck her that the latter was genuinely happy to be free of her husband. She raised her hand in a high-five, exclaiming, "Beer party!"

Saloni laughed as she lifted her hand in response to her sister. "Done! Only I don't think the boys are going to let it be a twosome."

Ruma laughed, feeling light for the first time since she had heard of her sister's broken marriage. "I don't think so either. Let's all go get drunk. Do you think Mitesh will mind being left behind?"

"We'll coax him." Saloni winked, a grin splitting her face in two. "And I'll leave it to you to handle Mamma. You're the rockstar, getting married to a guy she approves. That was a good one you pulled, by the way, the secret wedding. Hats off to *Daadima* and Akshay *Chachu!*"

Ruma laughed. "It was such fun, Sal. I had to marry Laki urgently or he wouldn't let me sleep with him." She laughed some more on seeing Saloni's raised eyebrows. "Yeah, I knew he was the man for me after we met the first few times. And here was Mamma, insisting that I should wed Bunty..."

"Ugh! I know. Bunty Vaswani of all people in the world." Saloni grimaced. "Where does Mamma get her ideas from?"

"Exactly. In the end, Akshay *Chachu* handled everything superbly. You were here and that was one of the main arguments which he used, about how you can't travel again soon along with a baby."

"Which is what I ultimately did anyway." Saloni winked at her sister. "So the plan is like this. I'm going to get myself a job first and then build my career from scratch."

"Splendid! Have you spoken to Pappa about joining his company?"

Saloni shook her head. "I don't plan to join him. If I go to his company, I'll be the boss's daughter. I'll not get to actually learn things at the grassroots. I'm planning to apply outside. *Daadima* agrees with me and thank God for that. I don't think I'd have managed to survive the last few days without her support."

"I think you're right. And I know exactly what you mean. Mamma teared up twice in the five minutes I was in the living room, playing with Mitesh. *She* needs to get a job." Ruma shook her head in frustration.

"Well, I'm giving her an opportunity to play fulltime grandma to Mitesh. I hope that keeps her busy." Saloni laughed.

The sisters never had a chance to have a heartfelt chat after Saloni's marriage. Saloni felt so happy to connect with Ruma. It was a good thing that Jaipur was not too far away from Delhi.

harmesh called Aarav on the intercom the Monday after the latter returned from Mysore. "Hey Aarav, do you have a minute?"

"Of course, Dharmesh," said Aarav to his HR head, "Shoot."

"I just interviewed this girl for the post of marketing assistant. She's good. Actually, she's way more than good. She's over qualified for the job too. Her only disadvantage is that she doesn't have any hands-on experience. But it would be foolish to let go of her is what I think. What do you suggest?"

"Do you want me to meet her?" asked Aarav, checking his phone for his schedule for the day. "Is she still on the premises? I have a fifteen-minute window in half an hour."

"That would just be perfect, Aarav. I'll send her over to your office." They chatted a little longer about the clients Aarav had gone to meet with in Mysore. He and Hiten had returned late evening on Saturday.

"Yeah, we'll meet at 5 pm regarding that. I'm going to take the contract, Dharmesh. It is bound to be challenging, just the way we like it, and I'm confident it'll open new horizons for us."

"Sounds good, boss! See you in the evening then."

Half an hour later, Hiten knocked on the cabin door before walking in. "Aarav, your interview's here."

Aarav looked up from his laptop to stare at his executive assistant unseeingly, nodding at the same time. "Okay, send her in."

"Good afternoon, sir," said a soft voice.

Aarav was turned to his right, facing his laptop which was set on the arm of the L-shaped desk he was working at. Without turning to look at the candidate, he said, "Good afternoon. Take a seat. I'll be with you in a minute."

Saloni sat on the visitor's chair, crossing her legs elegantly. She felt in her element, excited to attend job interviews. This was the fourth one she was attending in as many days. She was still biding her time, reserving judgement before picking up a job which would be challenging enough.

Dharmesh had been impressed with her and she could see that. And she had heard a little about *AC Events*. Now she was here to meet the big boss. It was lucky that he could fit in her interview at such a short notice. But the man was obviously busy.

She sat up straight when he turned his chair to face her.

"You!" They both spoke at the same time as steel grey eyes met melting brown ones. Saloni laughed softly. "Aarav Chopra! You head *AC Events?!*" She shook her head in a daze. "I must confess that I haven't done my home work well. But I thought you owned and ran *AC Properties*." She could not resist running her eyes over his handsome face. He looked good enough to eat. He must be thirty-one, if she remembered right.

Aarav had gone speechless after he realised who had stepped into his office for an interview, his heart thudding away like a drum. What was Saloni doing in Delhi? The last he had known—which had been barely a couple of months ago—she had gone back to Chicago with her husband and baby. And no, he was not hallucinating.

"Both." He did not tell her that these were only two of his seven companies. "What are you doing here, Saloni?" Aarav's voice was gruff. "I thought you lived in Chicago. Have you moved back to Delhi?" He shut his eyes for a couple of seconds, to gather his shattered thoughts together. Was the city big enough to hold the both of them?

Saloni nodded her head eagerly, not aware of the silky strand of hair which had escaped the knot at the back of her head to fall against her shoulder. "Yeah, I'm back home and so is Mitesh."

Was he hearing right? "And Manish? He hasn't come yet?" Aarav's heart picked up tempo, more than before, some deeply buried emotions fighting to surface.

Saloni gave a small shake of her head. "We aren't together." Her voice was small as she looked into his eyes.

Aarav sprang out of his chair as if someone had kicked him hard. "Oh!" He stared at her, speechless for a few seconds before saying, "I... I don't know what to say!" He loved Saloni, from the depth of his heart. But he had never wished that she should separate from her husband. "What happened, Saloni?" He fisted his hands which were itching to touch her. He wanted to hug her close to his heart and heal her pain. Why the hell had the bastard chucked her out of his life? Yes, Aarav had automatically presumed that it was Manish who had left Saloni.

Saloni shrugged, a deep sigh shuddering from her being. "Well, it wasn't exactly one particular incident. More like the way of life. I couldn't take it anymore. Mamma thinks I have failed. But well, it's just that I didn't want to waste my life away on that asshole any longer. That's why I left."

Aarav walked around the desk to sit on the corner next to Saloni. "Let me get this straight. Are you saying that Manish didn't ditch you?"

Saloni shook her head, more strands escaping her knot, a wide smile on her lips. "Nope. It's the other way round. I dumped him."

Aarav threw back his head and laughed.

And Saloni stared, her smile disappearing even as her throat closed up. He was the handsomest man she had ever laid her eyes on...

When she set her eyes on him for the first time at the tender age of seventeen, Saloni had been confident that they belonged together. Aarav had taken to chauffeuring her grandparents to work when his father Tejpal had been ill over a few days.

On the third day of Aarav's duty, Saloni had come up with a plan. She got ready for junior college and stepped down the staircase, calling out to her grandfather, Shantanu. *"Daadu,* my scooty isn't working. Will you give me a lift today? Or will you get late for work?"

Shantanu looked at his granddaughter with twinkling brown eyes, full of love. "Of course *beta.* I'll get a few minutes late. But so what? Let me take advantage of being the boss," he grinned. "Come along and finish your breakfast. And we'll leave immediately after. Ganga," he turned towards the bedroom on the ground floor, calling out to his wife, "Are you ready?"

Ganga stepped out, wearing a crisp cotton sari, wishing everyone around a 'good morning'. The three of them sat for breakfast as Vinayak brought hot *paneer-gobi parathas* with thick curds and pickles.

"No butter for me, *Daadu,"* said Saloni, moving her plate away. "I want to lose weight."

"But why? You are pretty slim now." Shantanu protested.

Ganga grinned at her husband. "The young girls of today want to be reed thin. Give me the butter dish." She took it from him and spread some liberally on her *parathas,* smiling at her granddaughter. "What happened to your scooty?"

"I don't know." Saloni concentrated on her breakfast, unable to meet her grandparents' eyes. She was not used to telling lies. "Some kind of starting trouble. I'll show it to the mechanic after I get back from college."

Shantanu shook his head. "There's no need for that. I'll ask Aarav to pick you up from college. He can drop you home and check out your scooty. He's good with engines."

Saloni nodded her head vigorously. "Can he do that? That would be awesome, *Daadu*!" She got up from the table to go wash her hands. Picking up a cup of tea, she sat down again until her grandparents finished their breakfast. The three younger ones—Ruma, Ryan, and Shaan—had already gone to school; her father Shyam had left for work early. And her mother Rati had gone to a nearby temple.

Saloni sat in the front seat, along with Aarav, while her grandparents sat in the back, just as they did every day. She was extremely conscious of his proximity and did not utter a word after she greeted him with a 'hello'. Her heart seemed to beat louder than the car engine as she surreptitiously checked out his muscular arm which was so close to her. He must be in his early twenties, she thought. He was neatly dressed in a pair of jeans and a white shirt. Her grandfather had mentioned in passing that he was in college, pursuing a degree in BBA.

The gates to her college arrived too soon for Saloni's liking. "I'll be done by 2.45 pm Aarav. Will you be able to pick me up after that, right here at the gate?" she asked. It was a wonder that the words were clear as she had to force them out of her parched throat.

Aarav nodded. "Yes ma'am."

Ma'am! Is that how he thought of her?! Saloni got out when the car stopped, waving to the three of them. She could not wait for college to be over when Aarav would come back to pick her up. She would set him right then.

Once in class, Saloni wiped her mind clean of Aarav and concentrated on her lectures. Time flew and it was 2.50 pm when she raced her way to the entrance, waving to her friends, not too bothered by the startled looks they threw in her direction. She could not wait to meet Aarav again. And they would be alone now, on the ride back to her home.

Aarav was waiting there, in the car parked to the left of the gate. Saloni opened the front passenger door and jumped in, saying, "Hi!"

"Hello ma'am," said Aarav, his eyes on the road in front of him as he turned the car key to switch on the engine.

Saloni placed her hand on his arm. "Listen, my name is Saloni. Don't call me ma'am." She removed her hand almost immediately as she felt a shock akin to an electric current as her hand came in contact with his forearm. Oh dear! Saloni sat back in her seat, trying her best to recover from the unfamiliar sensation, her heart knocking loudly in her chest.

Aarav turned to look at her fully for the first time, a fire in his steely gaze. "My father works as a chauffeur for your grandparents. I..."

"Don't be silly, Aarav. Do you really believe in such kind of social differences? My grandparents don't. And neither do I." She stared right back, her brown eyes glowing with youth and joy. She wanted to throw her arms around him and give him a kiss. She stared at the fuzz on his cheeks. His face had been clean shaven in the morning. Oh yes, she had noticed. But the fuzz was already there, barely a few hours later. She grinned.

"Is something funny?" asked Aarav, driving the car slowly out of the lane where the college stood.

Saloni shook her head vigorously. "Nothing." A strand of hair flew and settled against his shoulder.

Aarav turned to look at her, eyeing the strand which seemed to have parked itself on him for good.

"What?" Saloni asked him, following his gaze to notice what had happened. "Naughty hair," she laughed, brushing it off his shoulder, startled when she felt the sizzle of current again. "Aarav..." Her voice came out in a choked whisper, her face flaming with colour even as her smile disappeared.

Aarav slowed the car down before parking it at the side of the quiet lane. "Saloni..." He held the steering wheel tightly, looking straight ahead, afraid to look at the lovely teenager sitting next to him and was startled when he felt her soft lips on his left cheek.

Saloni's eyes were tightly shut as she pressed her lips to his rough cheek. He smelt good, all man. She opened her mouth to trace the tip of her tongue along his cheek in a small circle, revelling in the roughness of the fuzz, a deep sigh shuddering from the depths of her being. "Aarav..."

Aarav groaned, unable to move away from her, as if he was bound to her by an invisible cord. "Don't," he protested, a shudder taking him unawares.

"Why not?" she whispered in his ear, brushing her lips over the lobe.

Aarav moved away with an effort, staring at her in awe. She looked so young and innocent, but oh so beautiful! "I don't think this is right, Saloni. Shantanu Uncle..."

"...thinks very highly of you. You are his golden boy. Didn't you know that?" Her eyelashes fluttered rapidly against her rosy cheeks when she asked him the question.

Colour ran up Aarav's face. Yes, Shantanu Uncle and Ganga Aunty were too good to him. They had encouraged him to study, even planning to send him abroad to complete his fourth year of BBA and also get an MBA degree. He nodded now. "Yeah. But still..."

"Still what? Don't you like me?" Huge brown eyes looked up at him appealingly.

"That's not the point..."

"Then what is?"

"Saloni, you're a kid. You..."

"Do you really believe it?" Saloni challenged him. "Tell me if you don't like me; I can accept that." Her face turned mutinous.

Aarav was flummoxed. "But that won't be true."

She grinned. "Kiss me then."

Aarav moved back to press against his door. "No Saloni."

She leaned forward to press her lips to his, taking the decision out of his hands, almost lying across him, her arms going around his shoulders.

Aarav did not quite know what to do. She was innocent. He could see that as she kept her lips pressed to his mouth and not doing much else. With a tender smile on his face, he placed his arms around her slim waist and opened his mouth to gently trace the shape of her luscious lips with the tip of his tongue. Flames seemed to leap between them as they explored each other with both their hands and lips, forgetting the world around them.

Aarav came back to earth with a thud when his erection turned too hard. He gave Saloni a gentle push, removing his arms from around her. He pushed his shirt buttons back into their holes, surprised to notice that she had managed to open four of them.

He sat back straight in his seat, afraid of looking into her eyes.

"Aarav..."

His head turned of its own volition, his grey eyes running over her flushed face, her lips swollen from his kisses. Oh my God! Her hair was in a mess while her sleeveless top had ridden up her waist. "Saloni, do you have a comb or hair brush?"

Her eyes twinkled at him impishly. "Why?"

"Look at yourself in the mirror." He pulled the shade above the front of her seat that had a mirror behind it.

Saloni looked at her reflection with a grin, turning her head this way and that. She appeared thoroughly kissed. "You think that's bad?"

"Your family's going to kill me." Aarav groaned, laying his head on his arms which were crossed over the steering wheel. What the hell had come over him! How could he return the Malhotra family's kindness in such a fashion?!

Saloni took out a brush and set her hair straight, after pulling her top down to cover the waistband of her jeans. She dusted some powder from her compact on to her cheeks, pouting her lips to see if she looked alright. She could not help grinning as she realised that her lips were swollen and there was not much she could do about it. She had better get back home and rush into her room before her Mamma saw her and suspected something. "Stop feeling guilty Aarav. If anyone is to be blamed, it's me. I instigated the kiss."

He lifted his head to give her a sarcastic smile. "Yeah, right. As if I didn't respond to it." Noticing that she had brought some semblance of order to her person, he started the car and drove steadily, not uttering another word.

"Give me the keys to your scooty. I'll check it out," offered Aarav just as she was getting out of the car.

"No need. There's nothing wrong with my scooty." Saloni bent down to the level of the window and gave him a wink, blowing him a kiss before walking towards the lift, her slender hips swinging in an exaggerated swagger when she felt his hot gaze upon her.

Aarav swung the car around, taking a dangerous turn, leaving the compound with a roar of the engine. Would she insist that the scooty was not working until his father joined back on duty? Saloni was going to land them both in deep trouble. A smile flashed on Aarav's face. What delicious trouble!

Rati took one look at her daughter and snarled, "What have you been up to?"

Saloni stopped in her tracks, shutting her eyes for a moment, hoping that her expression would not give her away. "What are you talking about Mamma?" She worked hard at giving her mother an innocent look, unaware of the guilt displayed so obviously on her face. And then there was her swollen mouth.

"Saloni!" Rati stood toe-to-toe with her daughter, her hands on her hips and her stance threatening. "Did Aarav drop you home just now?"

"Yes."

"What have you been doing with him? Do you know what the time is?" It was almost five.

But then, Saloni had gone back home late many times and her mother had never objected. She did not realise that Rati had been waiting for her daughter to return since she noticed the scooty in its parking place when she had got back from the temple that morning. It was Vinayak who had told her that Saloni had gone to college with her grandparents. Rati had put two and two together and had arrived at an exact four—only when her daughter returned late.

"Mamma..." Saloni held her cheek, her eyes watering when she felt the hard slap which her mother dealt her.

"Don't you dare Mamma me." Rati's eyes spat fire. "Aarav is the son of our driver. Or have you forgotten that small detail? He is way beneath us in social status.

Don't you have any shame? I'm warning you right now. Keep away from him. If I get to know that you are spending time with him, his father will not have a job with us any longer. I'll have him dismissed without reference."

Saloni looked at her mother with stricken eyes. If Rati had threatened her with anything else, she would not have cared. But if Tejpal lost his job, his whole family would suffer. Aarav might have to stop his studies and take up a job. And how could she do that to him?

That was the end of her attraction for Aarav. She forced all thoughts of him and his kisses deep into the recesses of her heart. Saloni could not play around with his life.

She refused to talk to Aarav for a few years after that, even ignoring him when he tried to contact her. Yes, he was probably hurt. No, she was sure he must have been terribly hurt. But it was best to nip whatever feelings he had in the bud. She was sure he would move on.

What Saloni did not know was that Aarav had fallen so deeply in love with her that he would not let another woman into his life. He had worked harder than ever to excel in life and his feelings for Saloni had been the driving force behind the huge success he was today.

Saloni came to the present when she felt Aarav's touch on her shoulder. "Hey, come back to earth," said

Aarav, the smile on his face spreading into his eyes. He felt so light and happy after so many years.

Saloni gave him a shy smile in reply.

"And how is the little man? He must be what? Nine months?" Aarav's smile turned wider as he thought of little Mitesh.

"Yeah, in a few days. He has become very naughty and loves being pampered by everyone—the more the merrier." Saloni was proud of her little one.

"I'd love to meet him. Do you have any plans for Thursday evening? I'll be finishing early that day. I'll come over to your place to meet the little man." Aarav's only regret was that he could not go over to her place before that.

I would cancel an appointment with the Prime Minister if Aarav was coming home, thought Saloni to herself. "Please come over. I know that Mitesh would love to meet you again."

Only Mitesh? The expression in his grey eyes asked her the question without uttering the words and he smiled at the answer he received from her gaze.

Aarav decided—though he did not share the full details with anyone, not even Saloni—that she should work with all his companies, a few months at a time. She had no previous working experience. It would be ideal that she find her feet and the best way would be for her to learn the ropes of all the businesses before she found her niche.

Saloni received an email the very next morning from Dharmesh, to report for duty from the next Monday, as a Management Trainee with the *AC Group*. Her package was too attractive and she immediately accepted via reply mail, a soft smile on her face.

Later that evening, when Aarav had a few moments to himself, he smiled at the turn of events. He wanted Saloni to be a part of all his businesses, true, but it was not just because he wanted to do all he could to help her find her feet. There was another reason for his decision.

Aarav planned to make Saloni not just his life partner but also his business partner.

16

Thursday evening, Saloni felt like a teenager once again, her heart beating a tattoo in her chest as she looked at her flushed face in the mirror. She tried her best to appear casual in a floor length skirt of turquoise blue, handloom cotton with a cut that flattered her figure. She wore a sleeveless white button-down top which hugged her torso. She had brushed back her hair and tied it up in a pony-tail. Small solitaire diamonds set in gold decorated her shell-like ears. She wore no other jewellery. Carrying Mitesh in her arms, Saloni rushed down the stairs to the living room and let him down on the carpet. It was past seven and Aarav would be arriving any time soon.

She was not too troubled about her mother's reaction. For one, her grandmother was around and for another, Aarav Chopra was a rich and famous man these days. And thirdly, Rati's threat of chucking Aarav's father out of his livelihood did not hold good any more.

The bell rang as if on cue and Saloni rushed across to open it. "Hello Aarav," she greeted him, a welcoming smile on her face, not missing the huge stuffed teddy he held under his arm.

"Hey Sal, you are a sight for sore eyes." He smiled right back.

Saloni could not control the blush which stole up her cheeks. This was the first time Aarav had called her by the shortened version of her name which only her siblings used. Not missing the tiredness in his face despite her thumping heart, she said in a breathless voice, "Come on in and sit down. I'll get you a cup of tea."

"Don't go away, Sal." His voice was a whisper, meant only for her ears.

She turned to look at him, saying, "I'll be back in a second. Mitesh," she called out to her son, "See who has come." She rushed towards the kitchen to request Vinayak for a cup of tea.

"Who has come?" asked Rati, who was standing over Vinayak as he prepared dinner.

"Aarav."

"Why?" Rati looked at Saloni with a frown on her face, setting her sari in order before stepping out of the kitchen to greet their guest.

Saloni walked behind her mother, not bothering to give her an answer as she pretended not to have heard her query.

By now, Shyam, Ryan and Shaan had also come to the living room to chat with the guest. Aarav answered all their questions patiently, though his concentration was fully on the baby as he squatted on the floor near Mitesh. He nodded and shook his head to the chuckling toddler even as he chatted to the others.

"You sure have grown up a lot in the past few months, little man," said Aarav, his eyes studying the sitting baby with affection. He lifted Mitesh off the floor and into his arms, kissing him gently on a plump cheek.

"*Kaise ho* Aarav?" asked Rati, looking at him warily before her eyes darted to her daughter, though she could not read anything from Saloni's expression.

"I'm fine, Rati Aunty. And how have you been?"

Rati sighed loudly. "How do you think I will be? I suppose you know that Saloni is getting a divorce. I just can't understand today's generation at all. In our time, women stood by their husbands; they did not run away at the smallest excuse." She gave her daughter an irritated look. Her boiling anger had simmered down by and by when she realised that the circumstances were not going to change just because she did not like them, though she did continue to give not-so-subtle hints of her displeasure.

It first appeared as if Aarav was going to ignore her words when Mitesh gurgled, kicking his legs, reaching out to grasp a lock of Aarav's hair. "Oh, you haven't forgotten that game, have you?" Aarav laughed, rubbing his nose against the little nose in front of him. He spoke to Rati as he continued to look at the baby. "You are right, Aunty. Today's generation is different." He turned suddenly to give Rati a smile. "They are more solution-oriented and don't just sit around complaining. Don't you think so?"

Rati did not really know what to say to that and excused herself saying that she had work to do in the kitchen.

"Give Mitesh to me and have some tea," said Saloni, standing next to him.

He handed the baby to her and took the cup offered by Vinayak, giving the cook a smile as he chatted with him for a few seconds.

"You must stay back for dinner," said Ganga.

Aarav looked at Saloni with a quirked brow and said, "Okay, *Daadima*," when her eyes implored him to agree.

Dinner was fun as they sat together, eating their way through the *mutton kababs, chole bhature, machchli Amritsari* and *jeera rice*. There were *jalebis* for dessert.

Aarav tucked into his food, his eyes seeking Saloni's surreptitiously from time to time as she sat on the opposite side, between her brothers. His tiredness disappeared little by little as joy seeped into him during the time he spent in her proximity.

Aarav stayed back for a couple of hours more, chatting with everyone until Ganga was ready to retire. He followed her and stood at the entrance to her room, saying, "May I have a bit more of your time, *Daadima*?"

"Come on in, Aarav. Sit down." Ganga pointed to the recliner before seating herself on the bed. "Tell me."

"Er... *Daadima*. I..." Aarav hesitated, looking at her for any signs of encouragement.

"Aarav." Ganga held his hands in hers, a smile in her eyes. "I think I know what you're going to say. Go ahead and say it."

"I'm keen to marry Saloni if she'll accept me."

Ganga's smile turned into a grin. "You have my blessings. One word of advice though. I don't think she is ready to take the plunge again, not so soon after her disastrous marriage. And of course, you know that her divorce will take time to get through. It is going to be a lot of work for you while you wait around for things to move forward."

Aarav had seen the way Saloni smiled at him, her eyes holding a special dialogue with his throughout the evening. As for *Daadima*, the matriarch was not aware that he and Saloni went back a long way. He was confident he could win Saloni over easily. Okay, they might have to wait for the divorce to happen and then get married. But what was another year or two for a guy who had given up the hope of marrying the love of his life after waiting for her for seven years? Aarav had been heartbroken when he heard that Saloni had got engaged to be married the moment he arrived in India. He took a flight out of Delhi the very next day, not returning until he got to know that she had left the country to join her husband in Chicago.

"That may be true, *Daadima*." Aarav shrugged now. "But Saloni is the only woman I ever wanted to marry."

Ganga gave him a look of surprise. "Why didn't you tell me so Aarav? Oh my God!" She shut her eyes for a few seconds before opening them to look at him. "Why Aarav?"

"There was no right time I suppose. Well," Aarav got up to give her a hug, "You need your beauty sleep. I'll get along. It's late."

Ganga hugged him right back. "I'll be the happiest person if Saloni decides to accept your proposal. I know for a fact that you will make her a perfect husband."

"Thank you for your vote of confidence, *Daadima*." Aarav dropped a kiss on the top of her head before leaving the room, his hand lifted in a wave.

When Aarav came out from Ganga's room, only Saloni was in the hall, the others having retired to their respective rooms. Rati had gone only because she had presumed that Aarav had left and Saloni had not bothered to enlighten her. Mitesh was also asleep with Bindi keeping a vigil over him upstairs in Saloni's bedroom.

"So, you're joining us next week, right?" Aarav did not sit down.

"Yes, on Monday. Thank you so much for the opportunity, Aarav. I..."

He shook his head. "Why are you thanking me? It's what you deserve. The way I look at it, *AC Group* has gained an asset."

Saloni stared at him, wide-mouthed. It only went to show how much her marriage to Manish had broken her self-confidence. "Oh, come on! I'm a raw hand."

"All the better," he smiled. "We can train you the way we want." He stepped into his shoes, all set to leave.

"I hear that your employees never leave." There was awe in her voice as she stood up to see him off.

"You do know that it's their choice, right?" He quirked an eyebrow at her.

"But of course."

"I'll see you then, on Monday." With a wave of his hand, Aarav left.

Saloni stood for a while staring at the closed front door. Aarav had brought so much energy into their home, she thought with a smile on her face, as she turned to walk slowly up the stairs. He was on friendly terms with everyone, right from her grandmother, her parents, her brothers and little Mitesh. He had even spoken to Vinayak and Bindi.

She wondered why he was not married. And no, she was not going to think about their meeting so many years ago. That was in the past and best left buried there.

Anyway, Saloni could not wait for Monday morning to arrive. She would be going to work for the first time in her life. It was sure to be a challenge and she planned to do her best.

Aarav believes that his company has gained an asset. That was the last thought on her mind as Saloni drifted into a deep sleep.

Aarav could not stop smiling all the way back home. He parked his car in the underground garage before taking the elevator up to his penthouse.

Life could not get better at this point in his life. Saloni was single. She had a little boy whom Aarav adored. Okay, Mitesh had cried on seeing the big stuffed teddy. But well, that was not going to stop Aarav from buying gifts for him. And now that Saloni was going to work for his company, he planned to spend as much time with her as possible. Yes, *Daadima* had mentioned that Saloni might not be ready for marriage. But that did not really matter. He would woo her first, make her feel wonderful, do all the things that her husband obviously had not done. Marriage would happen if and when it was meant to. That need not stop them from belonging to each other.

He looked forward to seeing more of her.

17

"**W**ant to go for a drive?" Aarav asked Saloni.

"Are you sure? You must be tired. I..."

"Not so tired that I can't spend some time with you. So what do you say?"

"I say yes! Give me a minute, I'll get my purse and keys." Saloni ran up the stairs taking them two at a time and rushed back exactly a minute later, waving her purse at him. "Let's go."

Aarav navigated his car expertly through the roads until they reached a quiet lane and parked the car in a dark area below a tree. He turned to look at the silent woman sitting in the passenger seat next to him.

He felt a sense of *déjà vu* when Saloni pressed her soft lips to his rough cheek. It felt as if life had come around a full circle.

Aarav laughed softly, lifting her bodily over the armrest and into his arms. His laughter got caught in his throat when Saloni pressed her mouth to his, her tongue seeking entry.

Aarav groaned in response, sucking on her tongue, drawing it deep within his mouth, before tracing hers with his own.

They clung to each other, drowning in the onslaught of passion. Aarav pushed her short top out of the way to caress the skin of her midriff, while Saloni tore at his shirt buttons, her hands tracing the incredible breadth of his shoulders and chest. "Aarav... you are broader than before and," she looked up into his eyes, "Handsomer than ever."

"Sal..." He buried his face in her throat. He so wanted to pop the question then and there but her grandmother's warning came to mind and shut him up effectively. He traced his tongue over the pulse under her ear before drawing it over the shape of her ear. "You look as gorgeous as ever, all woman now." His hands moved restlessly over her back, one moving south to caress the curve of her bottom. He nibbled gently at her collarbone, pressing her closer to his aroused body.

She felt so perfect in his arms. He...

Aarav opened his eyes with a start when his cell phone rang. Shucks! He had been dreaming. He picked up the mobile which had stopped ringing, to see it was Hiten. That was when he also noticed the time. It was 8.30 am. How could that have happened?! Aarav pushed away his comforter to get up from his bed and stretched. He had never slept this late in his life, not ever. But then, sleep had refused to come last night as his mind revolved around thoughts of Saloni and Mitesh. He had finally gone to sleep at 4 am, trying to distract his mind by reading a book. It was lying there, face open on the bed, Jeffrey Archer's latest, *This Was A Man*, the seventh and last book in *The Clifton Chronicles* series. Aarav reached out to the other side of his bed and removed the book to place a book mark in position before shutting it. Keeping the book on the bedside table, he speed-dialled Hiten, going in search of coffee.

"Baldev!" Aarav called out before speaking into the phone. "*Haan* Hiten, good morning, tell me."

"You have an appointment at nine. I just called to remind you." Hiten usually left a calendar on Aarav's desk in the morning. But today, since his boss had not turned up at his usual time of 8.30, he had decided to give him a call.

"I'm running late, *yaar*. See if you can delay it by half an hour. I should be there by 9.15."

"Righto boss! Will do that."

Aarav drank his coffee before getting ready speedily and leaving for work. It looked like Saloni had thrown his life totally out of sync.

Well, it was time to move from simply existing to living, he thought with a smile on his face.

18

Saloni did not know where the two weeks had gone from the time she had joined Aarav's company. She was at work every day at nine am sharp and left by six in the evening. They had both Saturday and Sunday off; she had heard that Aarav discouraged working on the weekends unless an event was happening. She had been a bit surprised in the beginning as most of her friends worked late hours in their respective places of work. But it looked like *AC Group* ran on different principles. While in office, though the atmosphere was pretty chilled, everyone was dedicated and completed their work speedily and efficiently.

On the first day, Dharmesh had introduced her to Ganesh who headed the marketing division. "Meet Ganesh Selva. Ganesh, this is Saloni Malhotra, our new trainee. She will start work here and learn the ropes. I need a report from you at the end of two weeks, copy to boss."

Ganesh got her busy within fifteen minutes, after introducing her to the four other people who worked under him.

Saloni had been kind of sceptical about learning the ropes in two weeks as the HR head had suggested. But now, by the end of two weeks, she knew her work inside out, thanks to Ganesh and his team.

She could not help thinking that she had seen Aarav only twice during the whole time. And yes, she missed him. She mentally shrugged to herself. Right now, she was too busy juggling her hectic schedule between work and Mitesh. She was glad that her grandmother, despite the work she did at the family's foundation; and Bindi managed the little one between them, while Rati hovered around them anxiously.

Her mother, as expected, was not too happy with Saloni taking up a job. "Why do you have to work? We have so much money. Shouldn't you be at home, taking care of your child?"

"Mamma, wouldn't that be unfair to Bindi?" asked Saloni mischievously. "She needs the job."

"So let her work for us *na*? Who is stopping her?"

Saloni had laughed outright. "One little toddler. How many people do you think are needed to take care of him? There are you, *Daadima* and Bindi. I..."

"But he is your baby *na*, Saloni? Mitesh already has no father to love him." Rati sighed loudly, her eyes accusing Saloni for the father's absence.

"Mamma," Saloni hugged her mother. "Believe me, Mitesh never had one."

"How can you say that, Saloni? Whatever you say, I refuse to accept that Manish is so bad."

"I'm not saying Manish is bad either, Mamma. He is exactly what he is, totally uninterested in my baby.

And I'm so glad about that," she said fiercely. "He would never fight for Mitesh's custody."

Saloni realised that at the end of the day, she had to be clear about what she wanted from life. She was keen to have a rocking career and be a good mother to Mitesh. There was no news from Manish's end. Her father's company lawyer had advised that she needed to live separately from her husband for a minimum of at least one whole year before seeking a divorce. Just now, Saloni could not care less. It was a good thing she had not changed her surname to Chawla and all her identification documents, including her passport, mentioned her as Saloni Malhotra. That made life way easier than it would have been otherwise.

Just now, she wondered where Aarav had disappeared to. She did not want to ask anyone as she was still new and was not keen to proclaim that she knew the president of the company on a first name basis. An unexpected sigh took Saloni by surprise. Well, she obviously did not know him so well it seemed. Otherwise, would she not have known his whereabouts?

For his part, Aarav was juggling the work of two people to be available at his *AC Events* office, to be closer to Saloni. That was where he worked from most of the time. But he had to travel twice during that period—once to Jaipur and again to Singapore, both trips on a recce for the wedding event which they were putting together. Usually, one of his subordinates went on these trips. But since this was the first time they were doing a wedding, Aarav wanted to ensure that all requirements were met with. He did not want any stone unturned to make the event as successful as he could.

Then there were those minor emergencies which cropped up from time to time in his other offices, not leaving him any spare time. While all the offices were located in the same compound, they were in different buildings. He gritted his teeth and went through his work like a bull dozer, getting things in place. Normally, he took it all in his stride. But right now, his focus was to get close to Saloni and work was getting in the way.

Lifting his hand to check the time, Aarav saw that it was 12.30 pm. He *had* to see Saloni today or he might simply go mad...

All those years ago, after the kisses they had shared in her grandfather's car, Aarav had been devastated when Saloni disappeared from his life. For the first three days he had lived in the hope of catching a glimpse of her either at her home or outside her college. After that, until the end of the week, he had been worried that she had probably fallen ill. There was no one he could ask. But both her grandparents had seemed their usual cheerful selves. That was when he had concluded that she must be well.

Then what must have happened to keep her away from him? He had fallen deeply in love with the seventeen-year-old who had kissed him passionately. And Saloni must have felt something for him too, right? After all, it was she who had instigated the kisses. He did not think she was the type to flirt with any man who came her way.

It had taken a few weeks and a lot of heartburn for Aarav to figure out that he was probably waiting for her in vain. He was their driver's son. How could he have thought that Saloni and he could get together? But she had told him that she did not believe in their social differences. Then again, she must have also realised that her family would not approve, which must be the reason why she had cut off from him.

Aarav had always planned to lift himself out of his impoverished existence, taking his family along with him. But now, after the way Saloni kept away from him, he decided that he had to become even bigger than what he had envisaged. He studied and worked harder than ever, grabbing every opportunity presented to him.

Luckily for him, Shantanu and Ganga Malhotra encouraged him to apply to a few universities in the USA. He had even won a partial scholarship from the University of Georgia. Shantanu had helped fund the rest of his education. Aarav had accepted his offer only on the condition that he would repay every rupee which was being spent on him. "*Arre baba*! Okay, I'll take back everything once you start earning. Will you send your acceptance letter now?" Shantanu had laughed at the determined young man.

Aarav had gone to the United States to finish his BBA and then his MBA. He worked there for a couple of years before returning to Delhi for the first time since he had gone to the USA. He rushed home to his parents. His second halt was to be the Malhotra home. He would meet Saloni to find out if she returned his feelings before talking to Ganga Aunty about marrying her granddaughter. Unfortunately, Shantanu Uncle was no more. It was a good thing that he had lived to see Aarav's graduation while the latter had also managed to return all the borrowed money before the older man's death.

Half an hour after he entered his home, Aarav's mother Amrita handed him a cup of tea, saying, "*Haan*, I forgot to give you the latest news. Saloni is engaged to be married. The groom is an NRI from America..."

The buzz in Aarav's head had shut off his hearing power. While his mother went on and on, he did not hear one word after that. Saloni was engaged! He wanted to smash something, maybe even kill someone.

Aarav went and locked himself in the only bedroom in the house, not caring if he was inconveniencing the others at home. He banged his fists on the wall, his eyes burning with unshed tears. Why had she not waited for him? Saloni must have surely known that he was doing well in both, his studies and his job. Did she probably think that he was not good enough for her?

Barely twenty-four hours later, Aarav had caught a flight back to America, pleading an emergency at his work place.

Coming back to the present, Aarav called Saloni on her cell. "Sal, how's it going?" he asked.

"Superb Aarav. Where have you been? You've become a stranger nowadays."

"Miss me?" Aarav grinned as he got into his car.

"Hmm... yes," said Saloni before adding, "Terribly," in a whisper.

"I have a couple of hours of free time. Tell your boss that you're going for a lunch meeting with me and come down. I'm waiting for you in my car below the office."

"Are you sure?" Saloni looked around her to see if anyone had noticed the colour flaring up her cheeks.

Aarav laughed. "Well, I'm your boss's boss. Who do you think is going to question me?"

"Are we really going to a meeting?" Somehow Saloni did not believe it. Aarav seemed to be in the mood for fun or at least that was how he sounded on the phone.

"Are you going to ask all the questions over the phone or do you plan to step out any time soon?" He challenged her.

"Okay, I'm coming. Give me five minutes."

"Two," said Aarav, before cutting the call. He raised the volume on the car radio and hummed along with the song, closing his eyes and leaning his head back against the head rest.

Saloni opened the passenger door in three minutes, settling down before shutting the door. "Hey, what's up?" she asked, drinking in his striking features avidly. Just at that moment, she realised exactly how much she had missed him.

"Hey yourself!" Aarav opened his eyes to give her a soft smile. "So, how's it going?" he asked, starting the car to drive out of the compound's gates.

"It has been wonderful, Aarav. I'm working with the marketing department, with Ganesh Selva and his team." Saloni spoke for the next five minutes, describing her responsibilities before concluding, "And I'll be working with another team from Monday onwards."

Aarav gave her a grin, nodding his head.

"So, where are we going?"

"To my place, for lunch."

"Oh." Saloni's heart picked up pace. She could not help recalling their last close encounter. She wondered if Aarav was still interested in her. And how about herself? Well, he was a handsome devil and a successful one at that. She was definitely attracted to him. But... Saloni did not want to think too much.

Luckily for her, they had reached an underground garage by now and Aarav parked the car.

"*Chalo*, let's go." Aarav was confident of the fact that Baldev must have left their lunch on the dining table and made himself scarce. He had, after all, been clear with his instructions.

19

M anish was fuming as he tore open a packet of muesli and poured the contents into a glass bowl before adding cold milk to it. *It had all started with this*, he recalled with bitterness. How dare she?

It was more than a month since he had returned to Chicago after the disastrous meeting at the Malhotra residence. Thinking back, he wondered if his father had been too hasty in threatening Saloni and her family with divorce.

But then, she had refused to apologise, had she not?

What had he asked? That she prepared hot breakfast for him every day. Was that too much to expect? Was he not an easy-going husband? He made no demands on her. She had been bored in Chicago after their marriage. Had he not given her a child, a son at that, to keep her entertained?

Manish was so busy that he really needed someone to take care of his hearth and home. No, he did not much care for the physical closeness between a married couple. It was overhyped in his opinion.

The reason he had got married was to have someone to mother him. Well, some of the people who had moved to the USA from different countries, even Indians actually, had taught themselves to be self-sufficient. But Manish felt that he did not need to be. He had been a pampered child and it had been difficult to live by himself, managing his day-to-day life. Getting help to clean his apartment had been an expensive affair before marriage. And he had had all his meals at restaurants except for those occasions when someone invited him over or when his parents visited him. He gritted his teeth when he recalled how his mother had been all praise for Saloni, insisting that she would make him an ideal wife. Some wife! Saloni was too selfish is what he knew now.

Manish was due for a promotion. He would probably work longer hours. How would he manage his life? Who would cook his meals? Who would keep his house neat and tidy?

Even after thinking all this, Manish did not appreciate how much Saloni had worked at making his life smooth. He actually believed that she was selfish and ungrateful.

And the bitch! How dare she mention in front of his parents and hers—and her grandmother too—that they had not slept together from the time of Mitesh's birth? Did she ever look into the mirror? Saloni had grown fat and unattractive in Manish's eyes. And then there was the baby, waking up in the middle of the night and disturbing his much-needed sleep. Should

Saloni not be grateful, instead of complaining, when Manish had shifted into a separate bedroom?

Women!!!

They were such impossible creatures it seemed. But then, all those women who worked with him, the doctors and nurses, they were all so nice to him, treating him with respect. Why could Saloni not be more like them?

Manish was respected at his work place because he was good at his job. His wife did not think much of him because he had treated her terribly, having no value for her role in his life. But then, Manish's ego was too big for him to acknowledge this simple truth!

Forget Saloni! He had better speed up the divorce and get married again. How could he go about it? His family lawyer in Delhi had said that divorce, even by mutual consent, would be a long time coming as both husband and wife needed to live separately for at least a year before an application for divorce could be filed in a court of law.

Shit, shit and shit!

20

Lunch over, Saloni sat on a sofa chatting with her boss. It was Friday afternoon and Aarav messaged Ganesh and Hiten that the two of them would not be returning to office.

Saloni realised that she did not really know the man. What if he did this with all the new women employees at his office? She mentally shook her head. Of course, Aarav was not like that.

Suddenly, Aarav was on his knees in front of Saloni, his elbows on either side of her on the sofa. "Sal, tell me something." His voice was a soft whisper. "The first time I met you all those years ago... was I wrong in thinking that you liked me?"

Saloni's startled brown gaze found his, her eyes having gone wide. They had never spoken about it. She stared into Aarav's dark grey eyes which held such a warm expression in them. She could not help but study his attractive features, his broad forehead, his dark, curved eyebrows, his slashing cheeks, sculpted lips, the lower one just that little bit wider than the thin upper one, a hawk of a prominent nose and then those piercing grey eyes. His eyelids were heavy, with thick curling eyelashes that any woman would envy. After a complete scrutiny, she looked back into his eyes and slowly shook her head. "No, you weren't wrong."

"Saloni..." Aarav groaned as his body sagged, burying his face in her lap, his arms lying on the sofa, parallel to her thighs.

She watched in fascination as her right hand seemed to take a life of its own as it ran over his head gently, pushing back the silky locks which fell against his forehead. Her left hand immediately joined in the concerto, touching his nape gently. Her throat felt choked with the emotions of the seventeen-year-old whose dreams had been shattered in less than three days. But no, she was not going to think negatively. That had all been in the past.

It was the present she should focus on. It was obvious from Aarav's words and body language that he had never forgotten that day so long ago. Could that be the reason he was unmarried? But that sounded too farfetched.

Aarav got up to pull her into his arms, pressing his lips gently to her forehead. "I love you, Sal," he whispered in her ear.

"I..." Saloni moved away a couple of inches to look up at him with wary brown eyes. "Aarav..."

He pressed a finger against her lips, shaking his head. "I know you just got out of a marriage which you didn't want. Maybe it's too soon to have told you that. But I've been in love with you for more than nine years now. I left it until too late to tell you before. It doesn't mean that you *have* to reciprocate my feelings or even do anything about it. I just want you to know. *Bas!*"

Saloni's eyes went wide in awe. Could it be possible that another human being could love her without expecting anything from her? Aarav sounded too good to be true. "Aarav, I hope you won't think I'm being too selfish. I was deeply attracted to you when I first met you. Chances were high that it could have developed into something if we had had the chance to get to know each other. But unfortunately, it was nipped in the bud." A deep sigh shuddered through Saloni. "I like you, a lot. And," she smiled, "So does my son, it seems."

"Oh yeah! I adore the little man too." Aarav smiled at her, sighing at the same time. "I suppose it wasn't meant to be then. But I hope you'll let me get to know you more now that you are back home." He raised an enquiring brow.

Saloni nodded slowly, looking into his eyes. "I'd like that. Manish and I are filing for a divorce by mutual consent." She wanted Aarav to know about that. "I am hoping that it wouldn't turn ugly. But this is going to take a long, long time. I'd understand if you want to move on, since I can't say that I might ever want to get married again. I can't ever live under somebody's thumb, not after the lucky escape I've had."

Aarav laughed softly, pulling her into his arms and tucking her head against his shoulder. "Saloni! I love you and only you. After all these years, what I realise is that it's enough just to be in love with you. If you reciprocate my feelings and we can get together, it would be a celebration. Even otherwise, I never moped about it. But there's no question of moving on. I'm not interested in setting up home with any other woman. It's either you or no one. And no, please don't think of that as pressure. Not at all."

The atmosphere was too intense by now. "Come along, let me show you my home," said Aarav, taking her hand in his before walking to the French windows.

The whole of the top floor was his. Two-thirds of the area was his home while the rest of it, in an L-shape, was a terrace. Saloni's eyes went wide with surprise when she saw the long swimming pool, the aqua tiles glittering below the water, under the evening sun. There were eight lounge chairs made of cane, along the length of the pool, below an awning.

They turned left from the French windows to walk around the pool. Plants grew in abundance over the parapet wall which surrounded the terrace, making the ambience pleasing to the eye. "This looks so lovely, Aarav. You must feel proud of having achieved so much in your young life."

He shrugged. "I'm glad you like it."

They walked along the length of the pool and turned right. Saloni gasped in delight when she saw the garden swing which doubled as a love seat. It was set on a bed of luxuriant green grass. She removed her footwear to rush across the cool patch to sit on the swing, settling against the fluffy cushions with a sigh of pleasure. "This is heavenly," she declared, smiling up at her host who had followed her at a more sedate pace.

Aarav had taken his jacket off during lunch. Saloni could not help but notice the raw masculinity emanating from him now that his shoes and socks were also removed.

She forgot to breathe when he settled down next to her on the love seat. The swing moved gently forward and backward as they sat in silence, one with the atmosphere.

Aarav felt on top of the world, a soft smile on his face as he lifted it up to the fading sunlight, his tilted head resting on the back of the swing. After all, had he not bought and designed his home with Saloni in mind?!

21

Aarav and Saloni met regularly for lunch at his home from then on, but only on Saturdays. She never corrected her family who were under the impression that she was working on those days.

Those stolen moments with him were a balm to Saloni's spirit as they just chatted desultorily or went swimming, with Aarav making no demands on her. It was just two people spending time together while they enjoyed each other's company.

He also visited her home once or twice a week, to spend time with Mitesh, bringing him a gift every time.

It was Mitesh's first birthday. Ruma and Lakshman had flown down from Jaipur; as had Akshay and Sunita with their children. It was a family affair, an enormous cake cutting which was followed by a lavish dinner. The little boy had been in his element, loving the attention along with the dancing and loud music.

Saloni had put her foot down when Aarav had wondered loudly if he should get Mitesh a puppy for his birthday.

"Do you want my mother to kill me?" Saloni laughed at him. "And aren't you spoiling Mitesh enough already?"

Aarav gave her a cheeky grin, his eyes roving over her lovely features. "Babies are meant to be spoilt. And a puppy that grows along with him will make for amazing company."

Saloni sighed. "I know what you mean. But let's avoid that for now. I can't wait for the divorce to get finalised." She felt under pressure, with her mother giving her accusing looks at every opportunity. But it was barely four months since she left Manish.

That Saturday, opening the door to his apartment when the bell rang, Aarav smiled at Saloni, taking her hands in his and giving her a peck on her cheek as he always did.

Saloni looked up into his eyes, holding back the sigh which wanted to spring forth. That brief kiss on her cheek was too damn frustrating. Had Aarav not professed to love her? Did he not want to make love to her? It was marriage that she was not keen on. Right now, Saloni would not mind a tempestuous love affair.

She connected so well with Aarav. They enjoyed their time together, at work as well as during leisure. The first time she had visited his home, he had told her that he loved her and was okay with whatever she had to offer.

Saloni paused. Well... he was ready to accept whatever she was ready to offer. As far as he was concerned, she was not ready to give him anything, not with a broken marriage which was not even completely behind her. A small smile broke forth on Saloni lips as she came to a quick decision before throwing her arms around Aarav's neck. "Give me a proper kiss, Aarav," she commanded, sending him a sultry glance from her melting brown eyes. It felt so good to be close to his hard physique. Saloni revelled in the heat which swept up her body.

"Sal... are you sure?" Aarav's hands spanned her waist as he gathered her close to his body. "I won't stop with a kiss."

"Which is exactly what I'm hoping." Saloni moaned as she bit his earlobe.

Aarav's hand held her nape firmly as he lifted her face up for his kiss. His lips sought hers, first gently, turning rough as he felt her ardent response. Their tongues fought a duel even as their hands raced over each other, removing the clothes which got in the way of skin.

"I'll try not to hurt you, Sal. But I've waited too long for this," groaned Aarav, lifting the semi-nude Saloni in his arms before taking her to his bedroom.

He laid her on the bed and went on his knees beside it, checking her out with hungry eyes. She looked gorgeous, still clad in her lacy, black bra with matching bikini panties, a combination of shyness and invitation in her eyes. He removed the front clasp with trembling fingers, asking, "Do you still feed Mitesh?"

Saloni shook her head, colour running up her cheeks. Did he think she was still too big? She did exercise most of the days. Would he find her too fat too? Determined, she helped him pull off her bra, but crossed her arms over her upper body, shyness overtaking her need.

Aarav gently prised her arms away to stare at her twin mounds, his breath coming in gasps now. "You look beautiful, Sal." Aarav placed her arms at her sides before tracing a forefinger over the quivering tip of her left breast. It puckered in response even as Saloni whimpered.

With a smile on his face, Aarav cupped the breast even as he bent forward to take the tip of her right one in his mouth. Saloni's arms went around his neck to hold his head close as unfamiliar sensations raged within her. "Aarav..." she moaned, pressing her body closer.

"Mmm..." Aarav suckled deeply, his body clenched with need, his arousal throbbing within his strained briefs. His hand shaped the other breast, revelling in the softness as he squeezed and plucked the nipple between his fingers. He paused when he heard a loud moan, lifting his head reluctantly to look at her flushed face with slumberous eyes which had gone a smoky grey. "Did I hurt you?"

"No no." Saloni shook her head vigorously, her eyes shut tightly, unaware of the droplets of tears at the edge of her eyelashes.

"Sal." Aarav lifted himself up to sit on the bed, pulling her into his arms and holding her close to his clamouring body. "What has upset you?"

She opened her eyes to scowl up at him, her eyes almost black with dilated pupils. "*Nahi toh*. Why do you ask?"

He wiped a gentle thumb over her left eye and showed her the moisture. "You are crying." His gaze had turned sharp by now, studying her face keenly.

Saloni shook her head before burying her face in his rough chest. "That was just emotion. I know you'll never hurt me, Aarav. I've never been made love to in my life. Don't stop now, please." She traced the tip of her tongue over a male nipple.

Aarav buried his face against her neck, his tongue returning the compliment as he drew it over the pulse beating there, taking pleasure when it beat harder than ever. His hands continued to mould and shape her breasts, as he turned her around to hold her back against his chest, her lush bottom pressed to his tumescent manhood. Saloni's head fell back against his shoulder as she exposed her throat to his exploring tongue, whimpering with need when he nipped his way from her chin to her shoulder.

"Sal? I want to make love to your breasts some more. Do you..."

She turned her head to give him a sideways glance to ask, "Need you ask?" She pressed her hands over his as they fondled her breasts. "I can't have enough of your mouth on me."

Aarav did not wait for a second invitation as he bent down to clamp his lips to her left breast, suckling deeply, his breathing hard. He removed his mouth after a very long time to brush his rough cheek against the moist tip as Saloni yelped in shock. "Aarav."

He grinned, looking up at her without moving away. "Like it?"

"Love it." She buried her hands in the silky locks of his hair, rubbing her fingers roughly over his scalp.

Aarav moved down her body, his lips and tongue tracing the shape of her abdomen. He flicked his tongue over the thin white lines crisscrossing over her stomach, worshipping her. "The marks of holding Mitesh inside you. Was it painful, giving birth to a baby?" he asked, his head pressed against her body.

"The truth is that I can't remember the pain, only the joy of holding him in my arms for the first time."

"Spoken like a true mother."

Saloni could feel his grin against her stomach and could not help the answering grin which broke out on her face, only to choke when she felt his face rub against her vagina. She had not even been aware when he had removed her panties. Aarav was a smooth operator, it seemed. A fleeting thought crossed her mind. He was thirty-one and obviously experienced in lovemaking. Had he had many lovers? But the thought flew out of her mind the very next second when she felt his tongue probing within the folds of her femininity, a deep sigh escaping her as she accommodated his onslaught by widening her legs some more. "Aarav..." It felt so heavenly as she felt her muscles quivering with the pressure which built in her womb. She revelled in the touch of his hard hands as they caressed her thighs, not really giving a damn if he thought she was fat.

Aarav lifted his head suddenly, much to Saloni's disappointment. She had been on the verge of climaxing and he had stopped. She did not realise he had done that deliberately as he kissed his way over the peaks and valleys of her torso as he worshipped her breasts once again before kissing her lips. "Sal, you're the most beautiful woman I've set eyes on," he whispered in her ear.

"And you're the most handsome guy I know. Aarav... I need you inside me." Saloni rubbed her legs restlessly against his, her fingers clawing at his briefs.

Aarav laughed, saying, "In a second," before pulling off his briefs.

Saloni stared at him in fascination, her hand reaching out for his erection, her fingers gently caressing the shape. "You are big," she whispered, her eyes wide and transfixed on his length.

He pushed her back on the bed before reaching out to the bedside drawer when he remembered that he had no condoms stocked. "Shit." He moved to sit further away, his knees tucked to his chest and his face buried in them. "What an idiot!" he groaned.

She touched him on his shoulder. "Aarav, what's wrong?"

He raised tortured eyes to look at her. "I don't have condoms, not bought them in a while."

Saloni got up to hug him. He had not bought condoms in a while. She could not help but rejoice when she heard that. "Aarav, I'm fitted with a copper T to prevent pregnancy. You don't need to worry." She kissed him on his lips.

"Are you sure?" He looked deeply into her eyes and saw them lit up with passion. Pushing her back on the bed, he climbed over her to thrust into her invitingly wet core, settling inside her with a grunt of satisfaction as she expanded to accommodate his length.

Saloni was flooded by sensations as Aarav plunged deeply into her again and yet again, his tongue copying the movement as he kissed her, his hands pressed at her sides on the bed. She moaned when she felt his damp lips moving down her neck to her breasts, adoring them. She choked when she suddenly reached the pinnacle, the waves rising her up and up until she crashed, hearing Aarav groaning in synchrony as he climaxed almost immediately after.

He fell against her, his breath coming in deep gasps while Saloni clung to him, her arms tight around his narrow waist.

"That was simply amazing," she whispered in his ear. She protested loudly when he tried to move away. "No."

Aarav gave her a weak grin. "I don't want to, either. But I must be too heavy for you."

"You're perfect," she whispered, meaning it. She felt absolutely cherished, feeling all woman for the first time in her life.

A arav insisted on taking Saloni and Mitesh out for dinner that evening. They had made love once again, slowly this time and were still in bed. Saloni never wanted to leave Aarav's arms. All the years in between had seemed to have disappeared and she felt like a teenager in love. She felt so free as she explored every inch of his skin with her hands and lips, pausing to ask him now and again if he was enjoying himself.

Aarav hooted with laughter as he watched the intense expression on her face, his eyes feasting on her nudity. "How can I not enjoy myself with you in my arms? And in your birthday suit at that," he grinned.

"Now tell me the truth." Saloni pinned him with her huge brown eyes, her arms braced on his chest. "Don't I need to lose weight? I think I'm horrendously fat."

"Hmm." Aarav pushed her back on the bed, before turning on his elbow to study her figure, ignoring her loud protests. "Don't be so impatient. I've to check you out, right?" His grey eyes had turned mischievous as they ran over her body, staring a little too hard as her nipples turned hard in response.

He sat up to hold her face in his hands. "Your cheeks are a bit chubby and your lips plump." He bent down to kiss her before continuing, "And totally kissable. Your shoulders are slender and so are your arms. Your breasts..." he paused to study the said anatomy, ignoring her anxious look as he cupped them, "They are big and fit into my hands perfectly. I wouldn't have them any other way." He lifted his gaze to give her a quick glance so that she could see the honesty in his gaze, before he ran his hands over the slight swell of her abdomen. "This part could do some working on." He looked up to wink at her. "Are you aware that it's flatter since you began swimming once a week?"

Saloni laughed through her tears as she shook her head at him. "I think I'm falling in love with you all over again. But wait..." as he would have pulled her into his arms, "Tell me more," she commanded.

Aarav placed his hand on her vagina. "Perfection," he breathed, "Created just for me." He pretended not to notice when Saloni made a choked sound as he stroked her thighs. "Well, maybe not fashionably thin, but I prefer yours." He bent down to take a bite of her inner thigh, making Saloni groan loudly.

Saloni pushed him on the bed before laying herself across his muscular body. "You sure can turn a woman's head with your sweet talking, silver tongue. Thank you." She pressed her lips to the middle of his chest.

He rolled her on the bed, climbing over her. "My tongue can do better than talk. Do you want to know?"

Saloni's whispered "yes" was lost as he made love to her all over again.

It was a long time before they were in a state to speak. Aarav slapped her bottom gently, saying, "Get ready Sal. Let's go pick Mitesh up and go out."

"Hmm... in a minute," said Saloni, her face on his lap, too comfy to move.

They picked up Mitesh at 7.30 and went to a kid-friendly restaurant. Saloni had rushed up to change while Aarav waited for her to get ready, chatting with Shyam and Ganga.

She took a quick shower, staring at her reflection in the bathroom mirror as she towelled herself. It was the same body which had peeped out at her in the morning, and from the same mirror too, but it appeared different somehow, totally loved.

What had seemed like a fat, unattractive figure appeared svelte now as she turned this way and that, looking at herself through Aarav's eyes. Yes, his words had helped boost her confidence tremendously. But it was the adoring expression in his deep grey eyes which touched her heart.

Saloni quickly pulled on her sexiest pair of lingerie before donning a knitted jumper dress in teal blue which fell a few inches above her knees, the full-length sleeves covering her arms all the way to her wrists. Slipping into a pair of kid boots of the same shade, she applied some foundation and a nude lip gloss before clipping on a pair of gold studs to her earlobes. She had stopped wearing long earrings, knowing how her son loved pulling at them. Brushing her hair and leaving it loose, she rushed to the room on the side to check if Bindi had got Mitesh ready for the outing.

In a pair of denim dungarees and a red t-shirt, Mitesh looked adorable, with his hair brushed back neatly. "Ma-ma," he called out, raising his little arms to Saloni.

She lifted him up in her arms to plant a kiss on both his cheeks. "Mitesh, sweetheart, shall we go out?"

He nodded, grinning at her, a drop of saliva dribbling from his mouth as he clamoured to speak.

Saloni laughed, wiping his mouth gently with a tissue before lifting the tote bag which carried a change of clothes and nappies. "I'll put him to sleep later, Bindi. You take a break and don't wait up. You have fun watching TV," she said, before almost running out of the room in her eagerness.

Aarav looked up when he saw Saloni and Mitesh at the top of the staircase. "Wait," he called out, taking the steps two at a time. "Let me help you."

Mitesh held out his arms to Aarav the moment he saw him. "Da."

Aarav took the child from his mother to hug him close to his chest. "Yes, little sonny. I'm your Daddy."

"Da-di," lisped Mitesh, laughing, reaching a hand out to touch Aarav's face.

Colour rushed in and out of Saloni's face as she watched the two of them go down the staircase—the guys she loved the most.

They went to *The Grills King* at Gurgaon. Aarav sat Mitesh on a high seat meant for children, securing him with a seatbelt which came along with the chair. He fed him small bites from his plate, ensuring that there was not too much *masala* which could burn the baby's tongue.

Saloni sat there, smiling at them. It felt so good to have someone share the responsibility of bringing up a child.

23

Aarav was pretty excited when he opened his cell phone in the morning to see the Facebook update from Saloni. It said that Saloni Malhotra was 'in a relationship' with Aarav Chopra. The post had already garnered two-hundred-plus likes and a horde of comments. Grinning to himself, he speed-dialled Saloni's number.

"Good morning, babe."

"Good morning, Aarav. Miss me?"

He smiled as he heard the cheer in her voice. "Every second that you're away from me. So! It looks like we're a couple officially."

"I hope you don't mind."

"Mind? I'm on top of the world. Thanks, babe."

"Hmm..." Saloni rolled her eyes. Realising that he could not see her, she said, "He says thanks. For what may I know?"

Aarav laughed. "Are you picking up a fight with me?"

"Do you want me to? I can, you know. I'm sure we can make up soon after that." Saloni said the words in a whisper.

"Oops!"

"What happened?" Her voice was startled.

"Nothing. Just that my body responded with a little too much enthusiasm." He laughed again. "Would you like to go for drive? We'll take Mitesh and Bindi too. What say?"

"I say 'yes'. Oh, and by the way, what've you done to Mitesh? He keeps asking for da-di. I..."

Aarav's laughter was louder this time. "That's my little man. He's looking for me, right?"

"Yes."

"Then we need to go out today, together."

They chatted for a while longer before Saloni reluctantly cut the call as Mitesh called out to her.

Saloni's phone rang again fifteen minutes later. She was surprised to see that it was Manish. He started yelling even before she could utter a word. "What the fuck's going on Saloni? How dare you shame me like this on social media? People don't even know that we're separated and here you go and make such a stupid statement. I always knew you were an idiot. But this is beyond..."

"Shut up, Manish," Saloni snarled, walking out of the bedroom, out of her son's hearing. "How dare you talk to me like this? Just remember that I'm not your wife any longer. If you have something to say, just say it minus the insults."

Manish was so stunned for a moment that he was unable to speak. He took a deep breath before shouting again. "Have you lost it, woman? The whole world knows that you aren't with me now. How could...?"

"Isn't that the truth?" Saloni stopped him mid-sentence to ask. "What's your problem?"

"What's my problem? You stupid moron! I don't want people to know..." He was talking to thin air as Saloni had disconnected the line.

The house phone rang the very next minute and Rati picked it up on the second ring. Before Saloni could walk down and salvage the scene, Manish had placed his complaints with his mother-in-law. Saloni watched her mother's face turning redder and redder with each passing second.

Oh God! Was there no escape from Manish? And what was wrong with her mother? Could she not simply accept the fact that Saloni and Manish were no longer together?

She stood at the bottom of the staircase for Rati to finish the call. The latter banged the phone down and turned to Saloni, her eyes blazing with temper. "Is what Manish is saying the truth?"

"And what does Manish say?" Saloni asked coolly. She refused to be browbeaten by her mother. Those days were gone.

"That you have made an announcement on Facebook, saying that Aarav is your boyfriend?"

"Oh that! Yes, he's right." Saloni shrugged her shoulders.

Shyam raised his head from the newspaper when he heard his daughter's words, but refrained from commenting.

"Is he?" Rati snarled.

"Is who what, Mamma?" Saloni scowled right back at her mother, unable to understand her mother's question.

Rati noticed her mother-in-law walk out of her bedroom. "Mamma, see what this girl has done," she complained to Ganga. "She has shamed Manish by declaring that Aarav is her boyfriend. She..."

"Is he?" Ganga turned to ask Saloni eagerly.

"Yes, *Daadima*." A slight colour ran up Saloni's cheeks as she gave her grandmother a shy smile.

"That's splendid. I'm..."

"Oh, you understand the question now when your grandmother asks you. But you couldn't when I asked you the same thing. Aren't you ashamed Saloni? How can you tell the world that you have a boyfriend when you are a married woman?" Rati shook her head in despair. "*Kyunji*," she turned to appeal to her husband, "See what your daughter has done. She..."

"Yes, I heard the whole thing." Shyam admitted in a quiet voice. "Saloni, do you love Aarav?" He turned to ask his daughter.

"Yes, Pappa."

"Then it's fine I suppose." He turned to Rati and said, "Rati, Manish and Saloni aren't married any more. That boy is interested in neither his wife nor his son. Why don't you accept the fact and move on? If Saloni wants to marry Aarav after she gets a divorce..."

"I don't think I want to get married, Pappa." Saloni spoke the words in a whisper. "I don't want to be under any man's thumb, ever again."

"What are you saying?" Rati shrieked. "If you don't want to marry Aarav, then why have you declared that he's your boyfriend?"

"That's because he is." Saloni's voice was firm as she made the declaration. She turned abruptly and walked up the staircase.

Rati fell against the sofa, beating her hands dramatically against her chest. "What did I do wrong while bringing her up? Haven't I taught her any family values at all? Oh my God!" She ranted and raved as Shyam watched on in horror. He could not decide which was more shocking— his daughter's declaration or his wife's tantrums. He turned around to look helplessly at his mother.

Ganga laid a pacifying hand on Shyam's shoulder, shaking her head. "Don't you worry about anything, Shyam. It's still a long way for the divorce. I'll talk to Saloni. She's deeply hurt by Manish's treatment of her and can't stand the idea of being tied to another man, which is only to be expected. Let her be. She's so happy being friends with Aarav. I know for a fact that he loves her deeply. Everything will work out for the best. We just need to be patient."

Shyam nodded his head. "If that's what you think, Mamma." He gave a deep sigh, giving his wife a troubled look. "Times are changing and so are modern relationships. All I want is for Saloni to have a happy life."

"She's already doing that. Cheer up!" After saying that, Ganga went to sit with her daughter-in-law, running a pacifying hand down her back. "Rati, listen."

"Mamma," Rati howled, burying her face in Ganga's lap, "Where did I go wrong?"

Ganga sat there in silence, waiting for the storm to pass.

24

The next day at work, Saloni went and knocked on Aarav's office door first thing. He had pinged her on WhatsApp asking her to do just that.

"Hey!" Aarav got up from his chair to walk forward and give Saloni a tight hug before giving her a brief, but hard kiss. He locked the cabin door before guiding her to the middle of the room. "I've got something for you." He put a hand into his jacket pocket and removed a jewellers' box. Saloni looked at him warily as he opened it to show her the two matching bands of diamonds sparkling in their bed. "Just a little something for my partner," he said, taking her hands in his. "You get to choose which hand you want it on." Aarav looked into her eyes. "If wearing it on the left makes you feel that we are an engaged couple, then you can wear it on your right." He raised an eyebrow in silent query.

Saloni raised her right hand and let him place the ring on her finger and stared in amazement as she watched him lift her hand to his lips, kissing the finger which wore his ring.

"Thank you, Sal." He showed his right hand to her, with the ring box held in the palm of his left hand.

Saloni removed the matching band with trembling fingers to place it on his ring finger. She imitated his gesture by kissing his hand.

He pulled her into his arms, kissing her deeply. "I love you, Sal."

Saloni clung to his neck. "I love you too. And Aarav," she whispered in his ear, "Thank you so much. The ring looks beautiful." She kissed him under his ear. "Am I taking you too much for granted?"

He lifted her face up with a finger under her chin, his gaze smoky as it fell on her delicious mouth. "So what if you are? It makes me happy if you take me for granted. I want to be there for you, always." He kissed her hard before giving her a smart pat on her butt, turning her towards the door. "I'll see you soon at the meeting. Now go or I won't get any work done."

"Why?" She gave him a naughty look, tracing her right hand over the lapel of his jacket, pausing to admire the ring. "Are you suggesting that I might distract you?"

"There's no 'might' about it. You're already doing it. Do you want to leave or should I have my way with you, right here on my desk?" He wiggled his eyebrows at her, his eyes blazing with hunger.

"Are you challenging me?" She pulled his head down to kiss the corner of his mouth.

"Sal..." Aarav groaned. "If we didn't have that damned meeting in fifteen minutes, I would have done just that."

"Some other time, perhaps." She darted a mischievous look at the desk before lifting a hand to pat his manly cheek. "I'll see you later." She turned to leave.

"Do you want to go home for lunch?" he asked just as she opened the lock on the door.

"On a Monday?" Saloni laughed. "Don't make promises you can't keep." She blew him a kiss before going out and shutting the door behind her.

Everyone was already in the board room when Aarav entered. He took the seat next to Hiten before opening the meeting with a wide smile on his face. "Hello guys! Hope you had a good weekend, all of you."

There were a number of nods and "yays" before he raised a hand for silence. "I have two things to announce. One is that Hiten has been promoted to the post of General Manager of *AC Properties* beginning tomorrow." He paused when there was thunderous applause even as Hiten gave his boss a surprised and excited look. Aarav raised his hand once again before continuing, "Dharmesh, I hope you have the letter of appointment with you here." He took the letter from the HR head before handing it to Hiten and shaking his hand. "Congratulations Hiten! You have been one of the best executive assistants and you truly deserve your new position. The floor is yours."

Hiten cleared his throat before talking. "Thank you so much Aarav. I'm overwhelmed is all I can say. I hadn't expected this."

"Yeah, we've been planning this as a surprise for you since a while," said Dharmesh, grinning.

Hiten nodded before continuing, "It has been great working so closely with you for two years, Aarav. I've learnt a lot and promise to do complete justice to my new post. Thank you again, all of you." He spoke for a few more minutes before he was done.

"I'm sure you'll do a damn good job, Hiten." Aarav turned to address the others again. "And the next thing is a bit more personal. Many of you must have noticed that Saloni has made an announcement on Facebook..."

There was an uproar as all the staff got to their feet, clapping and shouting their "congratulations". Aarav sat in his seat, grinning from ear-to-ear as he gestured to Saloni to sit next to him. Hiten got up to give her his seat. Aarav held Saloni's hand as the rest of the staff continued with their revelry before two men from the canteen brought in a trolley with a huge three-tiered cake. The noise which followed was enough to split ear drums. Everyone walked forward to shake Aarav and Saloni's hands, offering their best wishes.

It was a while before the couple got to cut the cake. Saloni blushed a becoming red when Aarav fed her the first bite, before she fed him one. "Okay guys," Aarav called out. "A fifteen-minute break for the cake and *samosa* party before we get back to our meeting."

The catcalls and whistles blew the roof as the hundred-plus staff celebrated along with their boss and his girlfriend.

25

Saloni got the job of Executive Assistant to the company president. "I hope you don't mind being my assistant," said Aarav, holding her close to his naked chest on Saturday afternoon. They were at his penthouse and had just finished making love.

She raised her head from his chest to look up at him. "Why would I?"

"I'd rather you be my partner. But..."

Saloni shook her head. "I want to earn the job, Aarav. I'm truly glad to work as your assistant. I know I'm absolutely fit for the job. I plan to work along with you and learn everything. So, maybe I can get to be your business partner sometime in the future." She drew a finger over the shape of his lips.

"Hmm... I've been thinking." Aarav drew her finger into his mouth and sucked on it gently, arousing her to a fever pitch with that little gesture, smiling wickedly as he watched her eyes glazing over with passion.

She pushed him on the bed to climb over him. "You'll need to think some other time," she insisted, kissing and caressing her way down his body to his semi-erect manhood. She laughed when she saw his immediate response and climbed over to ride him.

Aarav grinned, his hands caressing her breasts before he placed his mouth to a tip and drew it in.

Saloni threw her head back, a long moan coming out of her lips as she reached her climax. She continued to ride him until he gave an answering groan when the orgasm hit him hard.

Aarav laughed when she fell against him. "You're insatiable, woman," he said, hugging her close.

"Would that mean I'm a nymphomaniac?" Saloni asked him in a squeaky voice so unlike her own.

"What?!" Aarav moved sideways to look at her. "Where did that come from?"

"Tell me the truth, Aarav." Saloni raised disturbed brown eyes to his.

"Sal, babe. What happened? We just made amazing love. What has upset you?" Aarav tried to pull her into his arms, but she moved further away from him, shaking her head.

"You said I'm insatiable. I..."

"But... Sal, I meant it as a compliment. Okay, I was teasing too. But it was in fun, not at all meant to upset you. If you're insatiable, then so am I. I want to make love to you a lot too. What does that make me?" He asked her logically.

Saloni sighed. "Manish called me a nymphomaniac." Her lips drooped with remembered hurt.

"Why would he do that?" Aarav appeared genuinely shocked. "I thought you said that he never made love to you after Mitesh was born."

Saloni nodded. "Yes. Well, I did approach him a few times." She turned red with shame. "Only he..."

"You poor baby!" Aarav gathered her close in his arms, tucking her head into his chest, pressing his lips to the top of her head. "He really starved you, didn't he? The bastard!" He ran a caressing hand down her back. "But that doesn't make you a nymphomaniac. You enjoy sex and so do I. I think that makes us normal, red-blooded human beings. Wouldn't you agree?"

"Are you sure?" Saloni lifted her head to look at him. "I do desire you, a lot. Is that wrong?"

Hot colour ran over Aarav's rough cheeks as his eyes glowed with joy. "I should hope not. If that's wrong, then I don't plan to ever be right." He grinned at her lazily, coaxing an answering smile to her face.

"I love you, Aarav." Saloni kissed him, her angst wiped out by his don't-give-a-damn attitude.

The divorce went off smoothly a few months later. Manish passed a few rude comments when he saw Aarav accompany Saloni to the court, but only within her hearing. Aarav Chopra was too big and too rich for Manish to insult him. She bore with Manish's comments stoically, not really caring as long as she was legally free of him.

"Hello, Aarav Chopra." Manish gave him a wide smile when Saloni stepped away to get some coffee.

Aarav nodded his head, no answering smile on his face, saying, "Hello."

"I hope you're able to keep Saloni happy. You know how it is. She needs a man all..." He did not complete the sentence before he found himself held by the neck, a foot above the ground.

"Do continue," invited Aarav, pinning the other man with his deadly grey gaze. "You were saying?"

"It's just that Saloni... will you please let me go? I only thought it fair to warn you and meant no harm." Manish's voice was almost pleading.

"This is the last time you take Saloni's name; do you hear me? If you utter it one more time, I'll ensure that you never find another wife to make a fool out of." Aarav dropped him, uncaring when Manish fell on his butt right down to the floor.

Saloni came rushing when she noticed Aarav manhandling Manish. "Is something wrong?" she asked, giving Manish a shocked glance as he got up from the floor, dusting his bottom.

Aarav tucked a hand around her waist before turning her around, saying, "Everything is perfect, now." He grinned as he bent down to give her a peck on the cheek. "So, how does it feel to be free of that scum?"

"On top of the world." Saloni grinned back at him.

"Good. Get your bags packed. The three of us are going on a holiday to Italy."

Saloni stopped in her tracks to stare up at Aarav disbelievingly. "Are we? When?"

"Yes, we are. Tomorrow afternoon."

They made a leisurely trip around Italy. Aarav had hired a camper which was the last word in luxury and they roamed the countryside, away from the regular tourist spots. Mitesh, who was almost two now, had a wonderful time as both Aarav and Saloni gave him their complete attention. They stopped and stared at every little farm and farm animal which came in their way. They ate local food, sometimes at farm houses or at little restaurants which served authentic food. At other times, Aarav cooked them simple meals in the tiny kitchen platform the camper was fitted with.

Aarav and Saloni made love under the stars every night, after Mitesh went to sleep. It was the best time of both their lives.

The day before they were to return home, Aarav sat outside on a recliner, with Saloni in his lap. "Happy?" He kissed her soft cheek.

"Never more so." Saloni held his hand with hers, pressing their rings together. Coming to a sudden decision, she removed the ring from his finger as Aarav watched on in silence. "Give me your left hand," she demanded. Taking it in hers, she placed the ring on his finger. "Will you let me make an honest man of you?" she asked softly, an impish smile in her eyes, confident of his unconditional love.

Aarav nodded, too choked to speak, shifting the ring from her right hand to her left, copying her gesture. "Thought you'd never ask." He buried his face against the crook of her shoulder, holding her tightly, overcome by emotion.

Saloni hugged him back. "How could I not when I know you are my Mr. Perfect?"

THE END

MORE BOOKS
BY
SUNDARI
VENKATRAMAN

SIMHA INTERNATIONAL
SUNDARI VENKATRAMAN
THE BANSAL LEGACY
BOOK #1
SIMHA
INTERNATIONAL
SUNDARI VENKATRAMAN

Rohit Bansal, the handsome and suave managing director of Simha International, is the envy of many—from a director of the hotel to an employee.

A thief comes up with a simple modus operandi, believing that nobody's really going to find out anything about the thefts taking place. But when a guest brings it to his notice, Rohit is determined to save the reputation of Simha International and ropes in a top-notch detective. Will Rohit be able to find who the thief is before time runs out?

The lovely and intelligent Tasha Sawant goes to work at Simha International as the duty manager. Her experience in the hotel industry only adds to the hotel's excellent service.

Tasha is attracted to Rohit and it would seem that he reciprocates her feelings. Well, the lady isn't looking for a permanent relationship as it looks likes she's already had an unpleasant experience. But then, what about the guy? Does Rohit want any kind of relationship with Tasha?

*Simha International is the first book in the trilogy called The Bansal Legacy.

Rose Garden INTERNATIONAL
SUNDARI VENKATRAMAN
THE BANSAL LEGACY
BOOK #2
Rose Garden
INTERNATIONAL
SUNDARI VENKATRAMAN

Interior Designer Jamie Scott from Australia feels a strange connection to Ooty, a hill station in South India—what one would say, 'a call of the soul'. Then there are those diaries that his grandmother had left behind. Jamie decides to go on a holiday to Ooty.

Rhea Bansal runs 5-star hotel Rose Garden International on oiled wheels, as its managing director. She finds herself at a loose end—as if there's no challenge left in her life.

And soon, the challenge walks into her life...

Will Rhea, with her broken relationships, be able to forge a new and lasting one, that too one that's interracial? Will she let anyone get close enough to reach her heart?

More complications set in though, in the form of a policeman and a politician.

Read the story to see if the high-powered businesswoman from North India who has settled in the South and the laidback artist from Alice Springs in Australia can have a life together.

*Rose Garden International is the second book in the trilogy "The Bansal Legacy".

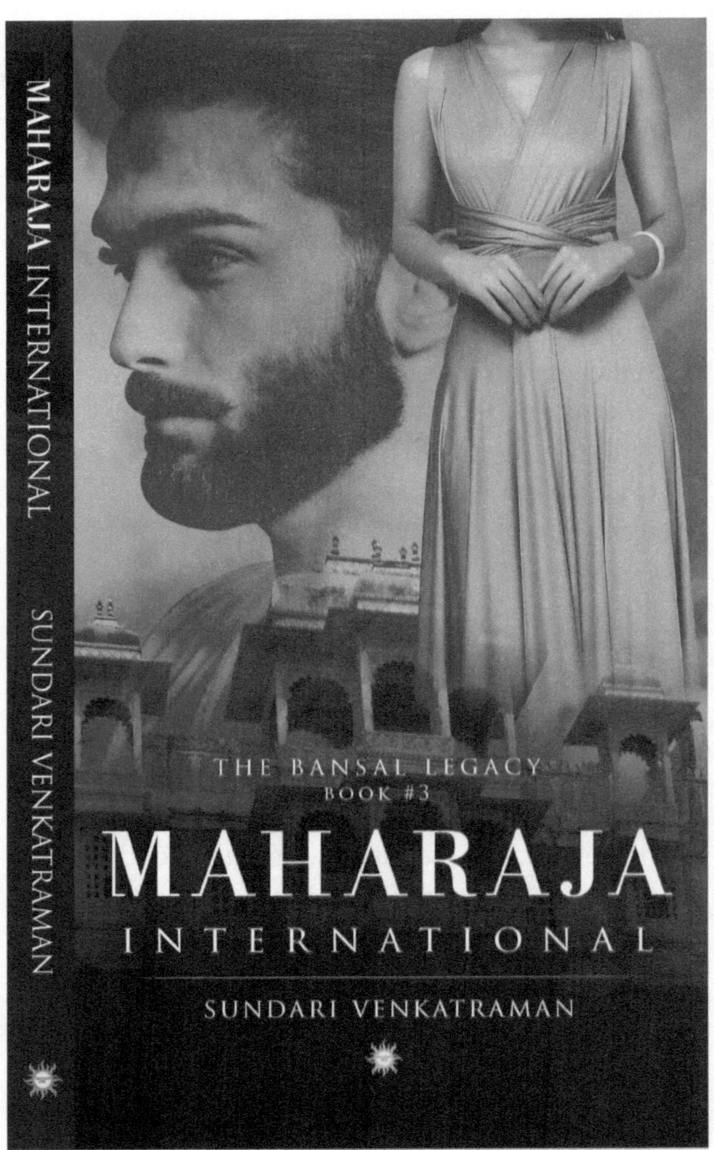

MAHARAJA INTERNATIONAL
SUNDARI VENKATRAMAN
THE BANSAL LEGACY
BOOK #3
MAHARAJA
INTERNATIONAL
SUNDARI VENKATRAMAN

itvik Bansal's decision to father a surrogate child comes as a total shock to his family, more because he insists that he needs no wife.

Two years down the line, Sia Rathod goes to work at Ritvik's 5-star hotel Maharaja International as the salon manager at Cleopatra's.

They connect instantaneously as sparks fly. After spending time in each other's company, they take their relationship to the next level.

Will Ritvik change his mind about getting married?

Even if he does, will Sia agree to become his wife as well as to be mother to two-year-old Aarya? Especially with the kind of past that she never speaks about?

*This is the third and last book in The Bansal Legacy series

Connect with Sundari Venkatraman here:

Sundari Venkatraman Books

Sundari Venkatraman Books

https://www.sundarivenkatraman.in

Author Sundari Venkatraman

@sundarivenkat

@sundarivenkatraman

sundarivenkat@gmail.com